This book is dedicated to my children. May my mistakes guide you through yours.

The Odyssey of Life: The Determination to Endure

This story is about my life. Every word of this story is true, and I have exaggerated none of it. It is, however, an incomplete picture from my fading memories and told heavily from my own point of view. From that perspective, some may argue or disagree with some of the events, but the hell with them. This is my story.

I am writing this story now at the age of 40 because, as best as I can figure, I have reached mid-life. These events that have happened need to be recorded in all their gory detail, for better or worse, and to honor those who lived them with me that are gone.

This is a story about life, loss and ultimately redemption. I have lived well, I have laughed hard, I have cried just as hard. I have loved many women, but I have loved only one woman the right way and with every piece of my being. I have and continue to raise my children the best I know how, I continue to try to honor my parents, albeit in my own way. I have partied like a rock star and have humbled myself before God. I guess you could say that I have done it all and now I am writing a book about it.

Chapter 1:

Early Life

My life when I was a baby until about 7 years old was reasonably happy, but somewhat lonely. When I was two, I would stand on the fence at the end of our front yard and shout, "Will somebody please come and play with me?". Of course, no one ever did. I would immerse myself in a fantasy where I could be the hero and was not alone with my imaginary world. Then, my parents bought me an Atari. The fantasy world I created was now quasi alive on the TV screen. This began my lifelong love affair of video games. With the Atari I could be Superman and save the day. Atari Superman is still my favorite games of all time and I play online from time to time to challenge myself to beat my time record. With video games my loneliness was not so lonely.

I can remember being so excited to meet my baby brother when he was born. He and I were going to be best buds, whether he wanted to be or not. Several times in our lives we would both want to be best buddies and both be our own worst enemies, with he and I the only ones to pull our asses out of the mire.

I knew my parents loved me and, at least I believed, would give me anything I wanted. I was always especially close with my Dad. After all, he was a big man whom I had no choice but to look up to and my only authentic example of what a man should be. He was exactly who I wanted to be like when I grew up. When I was young, Dad had a managerial position in a business called Executone, located in Seattle. The drive from our home to Seattle would keep my Dad leaving the house before sunrise and getting home after sunset most days.

It seemed my life was pretty good for a time. My Dad's mom (Granny) and my Dad's sister lived with us for a while before I started school. My Granny would watch me while my parents were at work. I am told that I would cry for Granny, not my Mom and, as a result, my Mom, somewhat understandably, became very upset and jealous at this. This would lead my Granny and aunt to move out and return to Missouri. This was the first time I can recall being sad over a loved one leaving. This also meant that someone had to stay home with me or place me with a sitter. The decision was made that my Mom would quit her job and stay home with me. This would likely become the first stone cast on their marriage that would cause the first ripple that eventually would grow into a huge crashing wave in my life.

My first real memory was when I was almost three. This was when my little brother was born. I do not ever have memories of being a small person, but I can remember being too short to view him through the nursery window and being picked up by my Godfather, Melvin (who was always simply Grandpa Mel).

My next real memory was a little preschool on South Hill in Puyallup, Washington called "Buttons and Bows". I truly remember being so excited about going to school the first day that I don't remember if the car stopped before I jumped out. Big Bird and Mr. Rogers had taught me so much about school before that I think I had it in my mind that it was going to be like heading to Sesame Street. They taught me how exciting this new adventure was for children, how the teachers were nice and sweet and would take care of you while mommy and daddy were gone and how being away from mommy and daddy was nothing to fear. Guess what, Big Bird and Mr. Rogers was right! Well, sort of, but I still think fondly of these memories of Buttons and Bows as one of the happier times in my life. Unfortunately, home life was nothing like "Buttons and Bows".

From what I can recall, my relatives all treated me with love and kindness, at least as far as I can remember. My teachers at school were all kind and good-hearted people (of whom I can still name my Kindergarten through 6th grade teachers). In fact, with one or two distinct exceptions, everyone in my early life seemed good and loving.

What I remember most about Kindergarten was not what you remember, if you can remember at all. It is not the reading or writing or learning the alphabet or numbers or nap time (I miss nap time). No, what I remember most about Kindergarten was the Gingerbread Man. The teacher hyped the arrival of the Gingerbread Man up for what seemed like a year, to a five-year-old. The anticipation of this sweet treat personified was the equivalent of Santa Claus arriving and, unlike Santa, I was actually going to get to meet him. Yes, my whole class was excited about meeting this person who is the embodiment of all kindergarten-aged children's fairy-tale dreams. Of course, the day before his much-anticipated arrival, I went down with the flu. That's right, I missed the arrival of the Gingerbread Man because of the arrival of a fever and copious amounts putrid vomit. Three days of school I missed in all. When I did return to school, almost as if to rub salt in this wound, someone decided that tiny footprints should be painted on the paved walkway from the basketball courts to the Kindergarten classrooms. To this day, I still feel sadness when I see gingerbread cookies. I few years ago I went to Puyallup and those yellow painted Gingerbread Man footprints are still there, mocking me well into my adulthood.

I have several memories of several people saying, "Look how smart he is." and "He is going to be a genius." or "You really should get him tested to see if he is gifted." Of course, I had no idea what any of this meant, I was maybe four or five or six when I would hear these people say these things. One thing about these things was consistent though: I heard people tell my parents very often how smart I was. Think about this for a moment: All your life you hear people tell someone, or even you, how smart you are and someday you will be an important person to the world. It in fact sets the bar high for that kid. Can you imagine the enormous amount of pressure that puts on a child's shoulders? Most of my adolescence I would spend years trying to become what everyone told me I was going to become and when I realized I had failed, I crashed. HARD.

While I never doubted my parents love for me early on, but I doubted their love for each other many times. I distinctly remember in the early part of my life my Mom and Dad having some colossal fights. Nothing physical or violent, per se, but I can still hear the smashing of dishes some nights if I close my eyes. I can recall crying myself to sleep holding my little brother when my Dad would leave and being confused as to what was happening. I think largely to avoid these epic battles my Dad not being around as often as I would have liked. This occurred, depending on which parent is telling the story, because he had to work late or was out drinking. Eventually, the fighting, arguing and mistrust would lead the two to a divorce. I was about 7 when the divorce occurred. Not long after is when my odyssey with God began.

The results of my parent's divorce led my Mom to keep the house and children, and my Dad got the RV and would only get to see his two boys every other weekend. Sometime after the divorce is when my Mom started taking us to church. It is my belief that she was doing this not so much for my brother and me, but mostly for herself. I think she felt lost as her marriage had failed.

Historically speaking, people often look for God when they are lost and hurting, and I don't believe my Mom was any different. The benefit to my life was that I was introduced to the Father for the first time. God and I would have a rocky start and rough years ahead. Some of the tragedies that befell my life I blamed on God. So much so that at one point I refused to talk to God and absolutely refused to attend any type of church. It would be years before I would allow myself to reconcile with God.

After my parent's divorce that I began to reject my Mom, and anything associated with her. It was my firm belief then that she was the reason my Dad left, and I would be angry with her over his departure for many years to come. My Dad and I were always especially close, or at least I thought so, and he was the one person in this world I wanted to be exactly like. As a result of this desire I would rebel against anything my Mom wanted. She would wake us up on Sunday's to go to church and I would start throwing a fit. She would want to have Bible study at our house, and I would do things to embarrass her, sometimes in front of the people from the church. I did everything I could to make her feel like crap so she would know how much I blamed her for making my Dad leave. Hindsight being what it is I feel deep shame and regret for the way I treated my Mom at this time period. I was a child and I was acting out against the person I held directly responsible for losing the life I had when I thought was happy.

When I was eight, my Father would move away from Seattle to Phoenix. This, like the divorce, changed the dynamic of our relationship. Now, instead of getting to spend every other weekend with my dad, I got to fly to Phoenix for eight weeks in the summer. This created several problems for me: First, I no longer had a steady father-figure in my life. After all, if my Mom was having problems with me, she could call my Dad and he could come to give me a "talk". As it turned out, his moving South created more anger in me which, in turn, was largely focused at my Mom. Now, she had no one who could influence my behavior, and we both knew it. Second, I have a younger brother who would do anything that I would do. After our Father, I was the next biggest influence in his life. Therefore, as I slid toward a negative life, so did he. And third, as a result of my increased rebellion, my Mom forced the church into our lives even more. In hindsight, I am not sure if this is true, but it seemed to me at the time that church involvement increased to every day of the week.

I began to develop a relationship with God and the Savior, Jesus Christ. The way my mind works is like a sponge and just like a sponge, I soak up all knowledge available to me. I learned all I could about God and Jesus and the entire history of the Bible and my faith in them.

However, because of my rejection of my Mother and anything she wanted, I did not want God or Christ in my life. My Mom was the enemy to me because, in my mind, it was her fault that my Dad left. As it was with my Mom, it would also take me years to reconcile my love for my faith.

Being a Christian was embarrassing to me, too. I wasn't a very popular young man in school, at either the Elementary in Washington, nor the Elementary and Junior High in Phoenix. After the divorce I began to cope through food. I would eat my way through my feelings. I was also molested by two different babysitters at this time, one in Washington and one in Phoenix. Then, I would eat more. Plus, no one ever taught to wear clean clothes or take a shower every day. This makes a person smelly and disgusting to be around.

At school I would be bullied at school for being stinky and eventually I became fat. The weight gain was a direct result of being bullied. Then, I would be bullied further for being fat *and* stinky. Most of the clothes I had after their divorce were handmade by my Mom, which were not popular clothing types or name brand, obviously. I would be bullied for these clothes, as well. Do you remember parachute pants? I certainly could never forget this tragically short trend. My Mom made me several pairs of these in the late 80's with the classic 80's materials, the bright colors with stripes, like a tiger's. I thought that these pants were going to turn the tide on the social terror that was befalling me. How wrong I was. Parachute pants had completely gone out of style by the time my Mom had completed my pairs. When I wore them to school not only was I continually picked on for wearing them, which cut me deep emotionally, I also grew a new hatred for my Mom because she made them. Of course, *she* was not to blame for these little bastards picking on me, but it was easier for me at the time to blame her then to stand up for myself.

In fact, some of the children came up with this not very clever song:

Look at him in his clown pants,

Running down the highway,

Eating lots of cupcakes,

Smoking marijuana,

Grabbing what he don't got.

Future songwriters they would never be. However, the damage to my self-esteem had been done and I still can hear their voices singing. Now, I was fat, stinky and wore homemade clothes. The fact that thirty-plus years later I can still recall the song that those little assholes sang should give you an idea as to how hurt I was. I hated these pants that my Mom had poured so much love and time into that I even tried to burn a pair. Of course (and thank God), I couldn't get the fire started.

Chapter 2:

Nemesis

There was a point in first or second grade where I tried to play sports at school. There was a kid who, at least I thought, he and I were friends from preschool. We both went to "Buttons and Bows", we both went to Kindergarten together. It seems, looking back, that every other year we were friends and then enemies. By the time we hit first grade, my parents had split up and I found myself in a bad place. This kid, whom shall remain nameless, had a chance to be a great friend to me. Instead, he was often a leader of bullies toward me. One incident stands out in my mind.

We were playing full-court basketball one morning before school. The teams had been picked and we were starting out and getting sweaty. Then, the kid I am referencing got "fouled" and was attempting his two free throw shots. I was standing on the outside of the key as he began his pre-shot dribble. I remembered watching a basketball game with my Dad and seeing this exact situation on TV. The on-TV player took his free throw shot and missed. The other players rushed in to rebound the ball and I would ask my Dad, "Why didn't he get another shot?"

"That's because he missed the first. If you make the first shot you get another shot, but if you miss you don't get a second one." My Dad explained.

Years later I would learn the difference between college basketball free throw shots and N.B.A. level free throw shots. You see, in college basketball if you shoot and make one, you get another (although, there are degrees of variables in that equation and really depends on the point of the game for the free throws) and professional basketball you get two, no question (or three if you are fouled while attempting a three-point shot).

This day at school, however, I only remembered the game my Dad explained to me. When the kid took his free throw shot it banged off the front of the rim and almost immediately bounce back to the kid who had shot it. This, it turned out was unfortunate. I pounced toward him because I was certain he was going to run toward the basket and go for a layup shot. As he saw me coming for him, he turned about 90 degrees to his right and said, "What the Hell are you doing?"

"Playing basketball, duh." I replied.

With no reply and no hesitation, this kid slammed the ball away from himself, returned to a square position at me, took a step in my direction with his left foot, cocked his right foot back and brought it forward to kick my straight in the stomach with as much force as he could muster. I had no reflexive defense mechanism at the time, so I took the full force of the kick in my gut. I immediately hunched over and collapsed to the ground. I started to cry as I curled into a fetal position. I was confused as to why this happened. What did I do wrong?

No one came to my aid as the bell for school to start rang. Every one of the children left for the school building as I picked myself off the ground and I wiped the tears away, dusted off my clothes and proceeded to the classroom. No one has ever said anything about this incident, ever, including me, until now. This child would be a point of contention for my Mom many times as he and I would be friend one year and enemies the next only to be friend the following year. This person would get his name spray painted on my Mom's garage door, see Chapter 7.

Chapter 3:

Al-Anon

My Mom struggled for a time after the divorce. She claimed my Dad to be an alcoholic and that alcohol was to blame for all their troubles in the marriage. She would go to

Al-Anon (a version of Alcoholics Anonymous for friends and family of alcoholics) and drag me to Alateen (Al-Anon for teens). Honestly, I was happy to go and experience something different and meet new people. One of these new people was named Chris. Chris was a teenage boy about five years older than me. I looked up to Chris because he seemed like a young man who could be my friend and someone I could emulate as I grew. During meetings it seemed like we would be friends as we always had things to discuss like video game strategies, since Nintendo was a big part of both of our lives. My Mom knew Chris's mom from Al-Anon, so they even tried to get together outside of meetings, but that discussion usually involved going to each other's church.

One Saturday, I was riding my bike around the neighborhood and I ran into Chris just outside of my school. Back then, school campuses were still open to the public. Chris was with a group of about five other boys, but they looked much older than Chris. I'd would guess late teens or early twenties. They were just under the awning of the covered basketball courts, just off the parking lot. I rode my bike past once, just to scope out the scene and see if I knew any of them. Nope, only Chris. As I circled back toward the group I heard a yell: "Get the hell outta here, fucking punk!"

Another, "Yea, kick rocks, kid!"

I didn't know why they were telling me to get lost. I continued riding around in the parking lot. "I go to school here. You leave!" I shouted

Chris steps forward at this point and screams, "Get the fuck outta here, right now!"

Now, someone who I thought was a friend was shouting and cussing at me. Something bad snapped in me and I said, "Fuck you! Punk asshole!"

This was probably the wrong thing to say. They started to ignore me and go back to whatever they were doing in their little circle slightly under the awning. As I circled I could see an occasional puff of smoke and I only assume they were smoking weed. A few minutes go by and I come close to the group when one of them yells. "Last warning, kid! Get outta here!"

At this, I stopped and place both my feet on the pavement and extended my right hand forward, fully lifting my middle finger in their direction. When they group saw this I heard some muttering until a thin blond, who I swear looked just like Steve Prefontaine, darts from the group and charges toward me. I tried my damnedest to get my bike going and get out of there as quickly as I could. I got about halfway across the parking lot before Pre's ghost lifted me off my bike and put me in a headlock as my bike fell to the ground. "Hey Chris!" Pre's ghost shouted, "I got 'em! come and get him for calling you a punk."

Chris and the rest of the group were there seemingly in seconds as I struggled to break loose of Pre's ghost's grasp. "This is what you get, bitch!" Chris says as he punches me full force in the gut. Then another. Finally a third and Pre's ghost lets me go as I collapse to the ground, coughing and crying. I hear someone say something about getting out of here. Then, in an instant it seemed, I was alone on the ground. My bike next to me and I was in complete pain.

After a while I got the strength to get to my feet, wiped the tears from my face, stood my bike up right, mounted and rode home. No one was there when I arrived, so I went in and washed up. Nothing had happened about this and I never would see Chris or any of those guys again. The only reason I can figure I got jumped was because they were smoking weed (or something) and figured since I knew Chris I would snitch them out.

Chapter 4:

Adolescence

All these tragedies in my formative years, as well as being bullied because I was getting fat and I was stinky led me to be rebellious and angry most of the time. The one thing I could change about myself was the burden of my faith in Jesus, so I rejected admitting to openly being a believer in Christ. Not openly reject, but I never brought it up either because I thought I would get bullied further. You must understand, when you are the target of bullies you will do anything and everything to not stand out and give the bully an excuse to target you. As far as I was concerned, to say, "I believe in Jesus, I am a believer in the resurrection and God loves me." would be the same as painting a target on my forehead. I still feel this some days today.

When my Mom would go to work, my brother and I would be left with a series of babysitters. The first one was two doors away and this lady was nice. Well, honestly, I was terrified of her at the time, but in retrospect she was just a disciplinarian. She had three daughters, the oldest of which ran away at least once before my parents' divorce. In time, my Mom would have the oldest babysit us when she didn't want to have us tag along on her "adventures" (I use the term adventures loosely, I just do not know where she would go or what she was doing). This would be the first time I would be molested. In fact, she molested both me, age eight, and my brother, age five.

While I was a believer in Christ, I was ashamed to proclaim it outside of my comfortable church circle. I did declare my faith by being baptized when I was nine. This did nothing to help me declare my faith and was more about me wanting some type of acceptance, on any level by anyone. You see, when you are bullied and picked on relentlessly at school you will do anything to not stand out or make waves. To do anything else is at your own peril. Already being fat and stinky and wearing homemade clothes, you do not take the risk of being a Christian to add to the laundry list of bulliable offences. I believe a result of these facts I had no choice to become a 'closet Christian'. That is, one who does nothing to celebrate their faith, except for accepted practices (as in Christmas, Easter).

Since my Mom was reduced to a working, single parent, I had a lot of time on my hands without an adult around after school. Instead of going home I would hang out at the park around the neighborhood or, when I did go home I would play Nintendo, instead of cleaning or something else my Mom would have appreciated. Honestly, my life in Seattle wasn't full of fun memories after my Dad left. I do not remember much, except the routine: Wake up, go to school, leave school, church, sleep, and repeat. That was essentially the life I had from eight to twelve.

Summers, on the other hand, were in Phoenix. Most of the time, we were at my Dad's apartment building when he went to work. The first year there was a teenage girl who babysat us, and, it turned out, she would be my second molester. To be honest, this molestation wasn't as bad as the first as I could keep my pants on with this girl. Although, I am not sure that quantifying any type of molestation as better than the other is appropriate, but that question is best left for the psychologists. The following year my Aunt would be the one to babysit us, when she moved to Phoenix to live with Dad. During the weekends, my Dad would try to do something exciting with us, like tubing on the Salt River. In hindsight, I think he was trying to make life seem good so we would want to be live him and not my Mom. At this, he was a success.

Another problem arose from traveling to Phoenix for eight weeks in the summer: boredom. The first summer I was eight years old and my brother was five. My Dad rented an apartment which had a swimming pool. Children were not allowed to swim without adult supervision, or at least someone who was over the age of twelve. What we would do during the week was wake up, play Nintendo and eat. And eat. And eat. There wasn't much for us to do while my Dad worked so I ate. I dare say that I put on over twenty-five pounds that first summer. To make matters worse, my Dad's favorite place to take us for a "fancy" dinner the night before we would fly back to Seattle was to go to Sizzler restaurant. The favorite meal my Dad would order for my brother and me was steak and all you could eat shrimp. Then, he would say, "Let's take the steak home for lunch tomorrow, and we should eat as many shrimps as we could. Let's make a contest to see who could eat the most."

Of course, my brother and I would completely gorge ourselves on those little, breaded shrimps. Personally, I loved dipping them into tartar sauce, so much so that it was more like I was using those shrimps as a spoon to bring tartar sauce to my mouth. We had to have had 10 refills of shrimp, each. This type of meal would be a mainstay of my diet every summer until I was twelve; overeating like that would lead me to overeating most of my life. While I have gained and lost weight in my life several times, overeating is still very much a struggle and has led me to several health problems. I am not blaming anyone but accepting my own behaviors, but also stating the facts.

Chapter 5:

Tubing: 1988

Tubing on the Salt River is a unique experience that everyone should try at least once. To my knowledge, tubing as it is on the Salt River is exclusive to that river. The term 'tubing' comes from the inner tube that you ride down the river. When we went there in the late 80's, you could bring your own inner tube (but, why?) or rent one from the rental place about a mile away from the launch point. There was also a shuttle bus that would take people from the rental to the launch point and pick people up from the end of the tubing portion of the river, then return to the rental place with the people who had finished. Naturally, heavy amounts of alcohol were usually consumed by the adults.

Our first experience on the Salt River involved myself, my brother, my Dad, a woman who lived at the apartment complex my Dad lived in (who he may had been dating, or casually seeing), a Devry student named Marty and his girlfriend, and another young couple who were very thin and whose names escape me now. I cannot recall which part of summer we went tubing, but I do not remember it being extremely hot outside. Not that which part of summer it is matters; Arizona is hot ALL summer.

We went to the river very early in the morning, though as it was still dark outside when we left the apartment. This is significant because, as anyone who has lived in Phoenix could tell you, if you are going to be outdoors, early morning or late evening are the ONLY times you would want to do this. If you find yourself outdoors in Phoenix, in July at 2:00 p.m., you must have done something horribly wrong in this life to be in that 100+ degree heat. In fact, as I think about it, I remember around 5:00 a.m. getting out of bed and running cold water on my face to wake up. This was before I discovered the joy in my life that is coffee.

Dad drove us from north Phoenix to the Salt River rental point and arrived in the morning that day. I recall it being daylight by that time and a long drive, at least to a child. My Dad and everyone else rented their tubes, and two extras for the coolers. Then, all eight of us hopped on the bus. The bus, which looked like a yellow school bus that may have been on loan from some school district, would be filled with people and inner tubes. The drive from the rentals to the launch point wasn't nearly as long as the drive from the apartment to the river, but it wasn't short either. The launch point was conveniently designated "Point 1". No name imagination here. We all got off and carried our tubes. We had to walk from the road to the river, across sand and rock. I remember when we reached the river thinking I would love to just jump in and soak up the water as quickly as I could. I was glad I didn't. It was starting to get hot outside at this time of day, but the river water felt like it was two degrees over freezing. It would take several minutes before we could get into the water and, by proxy, our tubes. Imagine being in the intense, Summer sun and getting into near freezing water. And, that water is flowing as a river does, and you will have some vague conception of the pain I would experience this day, going from one extreme to another. Our bodies are sometimes amazing, though as they seem to easily adapt to extremes, and it also seems that once you get your genitals into the water, you can adjust the rest of your body quickly.

The distance between "Point 1" and "Point 2" didn't seem that far apart, but that is probably because there were some extremely intense rapids (at least they seemed intense to an eight-year-old). After passing "Point 2" the river crawled to a slower pace. This, I would learn later, was why there are two launch points. The first states that there are "expert" tubing rapids and the second states that it is much calmer of a launch point. Leave it to my Dad to take the most intense.

After reaching "Point 2" I would also learn why we brought two coolers. The first had water, juices and sodas, with some light snacks. The second cooler contained the beer, wine coolers, Vodka and a mixture called "Jungle Juice" Jungle Juice is a terrible concoction that contains freshly chopped fruit, Hawaiian Punch and something called Everclear. This drink would inebriate even the heaviest of drinkers and my understanding is that Everclear is strong enough you could run your car's engine with.

The adults started drinking the items from the second cooler, with great enthusiasm. Keep in mind, there are six adults and two minors, both minors under the age of ten. As they consumed the alcoholic beverages, they got more daring. Between "Point 2" and "Point 3" there is a large cliff face that many people choose to climb to the top or face of and dive into the river. Marty had enough liquid courage running strong through his body at this point he decided to make the climb. As he climbed, the other five adults began to chat some kind of "encouraging" chant to dare him to jump. Marty didn't miss a beat as he jumped from, what in my best estimation, was a height of 30 feet. He would land feet first into the water, splash! Then, he would and reappear just as quickly as he plunged in. My Dad was next. Then, Dad asked me if I was man enough to jump. Of course, I wasn't *man* enough, I was eight. I have always had a significant fear of heights that still rears its ugly head from time to time.

When we reached "Point 4" the heat was becoming intense. We would grab handfuls of water from the sides of our tubes and splash them on our faces and legs often. Strong drink and intense heat are often bad bedfellows. The female part of the thin couple had had too much to drink and was passing out at "Point 4". Not good. Imagine laying across an inner tube on a near freezing river with 100+ degree heat and direct sunlight beating upon you, hard liquor coursing through your veins and you weighing in at around a buck ten dripping wet. This quickly became a bad situation for her and a worse situation for her boyfriend. This twenty-something now had the leave all of us at "Point 4", to get his girlfriend, who was in no condition, her and his tubes to the bus at this stop. A monumental task to be certain. Nonetheless, this man was able to rouse her enough that she became lucid, realized the problem she had created and carried her tube up the hill. He touted his own as well. Perhaps this scene is why I do not know their names today, because this would be the last time I ever saw them. The rest of us would continue to "Point 5"

"Point 5" we would eventually call "The Rock". This is because there are several large rocks at the exit point that are fun to swim around, jump into the river from or just chill out on top of. The Rock became a favorite point of ours that we would revisit several times over and, a few times, drive directly to and play upon some days in the summer without even tubing.

Chapter 6:

1989-1990

These years are very blurry. I cannot recall much except anger and frustration at the situation that seemed to be ongoing with no end. Remember, when I was in Seattle, I was constantly bullied and taken to some form of church.

My only respite was the eight weeks in Phoenix each summer. I do have a memory of my tenth birthday cake/party. It was at the pool at the apartment complex my Dad was staying at in Phoenix. He had gathered of few of the other renters of the complex and I remember what may have been four other children. The biggest memory of this birthday was the cake. It was in the shape of a woman and she was completely nude. I guess my Dad figured I was old enough, at ten, to see this type of adult material.

One highlight from this summer was crank calls. We discovered that we could order a pizza from whatever pizza company and have it delivered to an apartment where we weren't. The delivery driver would show up with three or four pizzas that we ordered and knock on the door and we would wait and watch. We always got a huge laugh at watching the delivery driver get pissed when no one was in the apartment. It was after several of these calls we realized what we were doing was causing someone else pain. The driver shouted one time, "Ha ha, very funny you assholes! I have to pay for these pizzas now!" We stopped after that.

Monsoon season in Arizona can produce some awful dust and rain storms. Dad had taken us to see 'Total Recall' in the summer of 1990 at the West Valley Mall Theater (its now a Wal-Mart) and, while we were watching, an evening monsoon kicked up and took the power out. It was sort of scary of us to be in the middle of an action film of that kind and suddenly be in a pitch-black theater. The emergency lights kicked on within a minute and all was well. The manager gave us all passes to come back tomorrow to finish the film.

Also, Dad took us to a drive-in to see Tim Burton's version of 'Batman". Another monsoon came while we were watching the movie, but this time it was awesome. There is a scene where Batman is taking Vicky Vale to the Batcave and the scene switches between the Batmobile driving toward the screen to it driving away. Just as the scene switched a bolt of lightening flashed to the right of the screen, giving the appearance that the lightening came from the Batmobile. We all looked at each other and said, "Did you see that?!?" All God right there.

Chapter 7:

1991

After the summer when I turned twelve, I had decided that I had enough of my life being the way it was. When I returned from me and my brothers yearly summer visit to Arizona back to Seattle in August, I was going to take matters into my hands. The anger and hate that had been growing within me had begun to boil over and I spiraled downward quickly. I got my hands on some spray paint and wrote some obscene words on my Mom's garage door, as well as the name of one of my tormentors from school. I remember I wanted him to see it and know what I had done. I don't know if he ever saw it, but my Mom sure did. The ass whooping I would receive for this was well deserved. I got a hold of a pocketknife and started to damage some trees in the neighborhood. Occasionally, I would get caught and get in a bit of trouble, but nothing that would be considered extremely serious; no criminal record. When school started in September I would not go very often. I somehow convinced my Mom to allow me to stay home each time, kind of getting a permission from her, of sorts. I would usually feign illness after she had left for work, call her and tell her and convince her I had to stay home. At this point I was tired of being made fun of for being fat and stinky and wearing homemade, dirty clothes. Going to school meant I would be bullied, every single day. This was a different time than today; teachers couldn't or wouldn't do much to stop these problems. Perhaps they knew and just turned a blind eye. Either way, I felt so very alone. That said, there was one person who would somehow take notice: the school's counselor. Honestly, this woman may very well have saved my life. If she ever reads this, Mrs. Bryant, please know that I love you for how you saved me and my brother.

Even with the school's counselor trying so hard to salvage me, I was in open rebellion and was determined to be allowed to leave and move to Phoenix. From September to around Halloween that year, if I went to school 3 days a week I was there more frequent than usual. In all likelihood, I went 1 or 2 days at most. It wasn't until the school counselor called my Dad to say that I wasn't going to pass the 6th grade that things started to change. I want to say this plainly, though, I was not our running the streets or causing trouble as some would think. I would call my Mom at work and tell her some other bullshit, like I have diarrhea or I puked and she would tell me I can stay home. Then, I would play Nintendo all day. Mom eventually figured I was playing video games and started taking the controllers to work with her. She left the light zapper and, even though it wasn't my favorite game, I still tried to play 'Duck Hunt'. Our game cartridge was a 'Super Mario Bros.' and 'Duck Hunt' combo and you needed a controller to select the 'Duck Hunt' option. No games for me, at least until I asked a friend down the street if I could borrow his controller every once in a while.

I do not know the details of what had occurred between the adults during the period after Halloween and a week after Thanksgiving, but I felt there had been a change had been happening and decisions about me were being made. Whenever a major change is on the horizon it usually is noticeable quite early. It can become palpable with a life-changing decision being made, often without a word being spoken. People's attitudes toward you will be noticeably different. Perhaps, God in his mysteries has created us with the fore-knowledge to feel these major changes before they come to fruition. I actually realized that a change had occurred on a day I actually showed up for school.

The 'family meeting' that went on between my Mom, brother and myself on our living room floor. There, filled with tears and eyes puffy, my Mom told us that she had made the decision that we needed to go to live with our Father in Phoenix. She would be saying things like "it's not because I do not love you, but *because* I love you that you need to be with your father" and "things will be better for you both there". I knew, but never said it, that this was a result of my own personal rebellion. We would be packing our things and flying to Phoenix the day after Christmas. What was in store for us in Arizona was both exciting and horrifying. What we found was different than we expected, and this newfound existence would alter the course of my history and, eventually, my odyssey with God.

My sixth-grade teacher liked to let the students share any good news every Monday morning. After the family meeting with Mom, I actually showed for school and, when the teacher asked for any one with good news to share I raise my hand as quickly as I could. To me, I felt like I have a bubble in my through the size of a baseball and I need to get this out before I choke. Of course, I had to wait for the teacher to go down her list of favorites who wanted to share how they got a new sweater, or went fishing over the weekend. I have life changing news to share and could give a shit about your fucking turtle neck or you and your dad catching a rainbow trout out of some god-awful man-made lake. Finally, when I got my turn, I jumped right out of my seat. It seemed to me that everyone was slightly shocked by this and I had a captive audience. I said, "All's I know is I am leaving after Christmas and flying to Phoenix."

My teacher had a look on her face like I had just revealed some God-awful truth that wasn't for public knowledge. I'm sorry, Mrs. Teacher, but I was feeling like I was going to burst if I didn't just let the whole world know. After a moment she said, "For those of you who do not know, he and his brother will be moving to Phoenix to live with his Dad after the Winter break."

Now, I was the one with a dumb look on my face. I didn't think she, or anyone outside my family was aware of this. I expected her to have some follow up questions for me, but there were none. I slowly sank back into my chair and thought about what she just said a moment, then she continued, "We are all very happy and excited for you in this huge life-changing event and wish you the best."

"Thank you." was all I could muster. The wind had been completely knocked out of my sails and I am back to being unimportant. Sorry I couldn't share about some football game I went to or hike my family went on. No, my sharing moment was dismissed because she already knew I was moving. Here was a final moment that summed up my entire life at this shit-show elementary school: being bullied by a teacher! After this, I decided I truly did not give a fuck about being at this school or this town and was ready to get the hell on to Phoenix.

As an adult I have realized something: When you grow up in the same area your entire life, you have friends that last a lifetime. I see it as a teacher; my students have been around the majority of their peers their entire lives and know how each other acts and tolerates them. Sure, there is an occasional fight, but nothing a few fists don't solve. Having moved one thousand miles away from the people I had grown up with until I was twelve, in 1991, meant that I would never communicate with anyone from these early years of my life. Now, having grown up in Phoenix and having very few friends I still communicate with I realize that I missed out on life-long friends that my peers have. Another casualty of my parents' divorce.

Chapter 8:

Travel

Moving to Phoenix was exciting. I was twelve at the time and my brother nine. We had traveled this flight many times alone, but this would be the last time. No round-trip ticket. This was also the day after Christmas, but it didn't seem nearly as busy as you would think. We packed all we could fit in to two suitcases and one large cargo box each. What we left behind, it would turn out, was a life that I had long forgotten and sometimes wished I hadn't totally left the way I did. To explain, Seattle is a different world compared to Phoenix, and some days (especially during the summer) I miss Seattle. More recently, I learned that many of the toys (which seemed so important at the young age I was) that I left behind are extremely valuable in today's market. When my Mom sold her house, she threw most of these things out. That, of course, is a different story.

My last night in Seattle, which was Christmas night, I can remember praying to God. I asked God to bless our flight and keep my brother and me safe. Even though we had flown this flight many times before this, I was terrified that something was going to happen to the plane. I remember that I saw the film, "La Bamba" a week before and I was suddenly and irrationally scared to fly. Of course, when the day of the flight came, I got on the airplane with my brother and we arrived safely.

When my brother and I were finally in the airplane that would begin our first leg of our journey to Phoenix I asked my brother for a favor: if I saw ANY cuss words I gave him permission to slap my face. I had an awful potty mouth at twelve and My Dad would want to whip my ass with his belt if I cussed in front of him. This was a big problem for me as cussing had become a habit and, like any other habit, would take a new routine to break.

The three days after Christmas that year was a weird time in my life. We flew from Seattle to Phoenix with an hour layover in Las Vegas. Vegas, it would turn out, I would return to in a day, but by driving. After we arrived in Phoenix, our Dad and his girlfriend (at the time) met us at the airport with hugs and much enthusiasm. We were taken to their home in west Phoenix, a cozy 4-bedroom, 2 baths detached home, with a pool. The layout was 1 Master with 1 bath, 2 bedrooms and the other bath, all of which were down the hallway from the entry/main living room. The kitchen and dining room were through an open walkway from the living room. A doorway separated the fourth bedroom (which was a converted carport) from the dining room. Also, through the dining room you could walk through an open area to an enclosed "Arizona Room". The "Arizona Room" also connected to the back area, where the water heater and washer/dryer was, as well as a spare refrigerator and stand-alone freezer. The back area had a sliding glass door which, when opened, led to a patio/grass area and then a chain-link fence that separated the backyard from the pool.

Up until this point, my family had only been the two of us, and whichever of our parents that we were with at the time. Now, there were many people living in this house. First, my brother and I were the most recent additions. Then, my Dad and his girlfriend and her daughter (my Dad and his girlfriend bought this house together). Next, from my Dad's first marriage (not my Mom) he had moved in his former brother-in-law, his wife, and their three sons. Finally, there was a man living there while working for my Dad's business and trying to get on his feet. This meant that the total people living in my new home was 11. Now if you are thinking 'holy crap', you would be right. None of that mattered to me at the time. What mattered was that I was home and exactly where I wanted to be.

The next day (December 27) my Dad announces that we are going to Vegas and he and his girlfriend were getting married. So, a day after I had flown from Seattle to Las Vegas to Phoenix, we were going back to Vegas but this time, we drove. We stayed at the 'Circus, Circus' and they got married at a chapel across the street. I was unable to be there because I ate a burger that I should not have ate on the way to Vegas and had gotten food poisoning. I was up vomiting all night after we got checked in and most of the morning. Seriously, I was up the night before the wedding puking everything my system had, as if *I* was the one about to get married.

Once everyone had left and went to the chapel, God said to me that I needed to get my butt out of bed and make it to the chapel. I mustered whatever strength I could and I got dressed and, only by the grace of God, stumbled across the street to get there just as they were leaving the chapel. I remember my now step-Mom saying something along the lines of "Oh my God, what are you doing? You need to be back in bed!"

To which I responded, "This is too important. I needed to be here." Unfortunately, I had gotten there much too late. There was nothing I could do, I had missed my Dad's wedding. As if a constant reminder for me not making it, their wedding photo would be visible plain as day to anyone who could walk through the front door of the house. All too often many people would ask why I wasn't in the photo and I would have to relive the story, every single time I walked through the front door.

Years would pass before I actually considered that, when I left Seattle, I was absolutely leaving behind a true loss: any type of relationship with my Mom's parents. My grandparents were truly great people. My grandfather, a World War II naval veteran turned apple and pear farmer and my grandmother was just about the most loving woman I had ever met. She was an artist and musician, who painted and tried (unsuccessfully) to teach me the piano. The last time I saw my grandmother she was bedridden with Alzheimer's Disease and she barely recognized me. She was unable to speak, but despite this she did smile at me when she saw my face. She passed away in 2001. My grandfather lived awhile longer, but the years of farming took their toll and toward the end of his life he could no longer tend the farm. My memories of him were a big, burly man who always had jean overalls. The last I saw him was Thanksgiving 2004 and he was a shadow of his former self. He had lost so much weight that I hardly recognized him. He would pass away the following summer of 2005. The loss I felt at their passing cannot accurately be put into words. I did not bring myself to attend either of their funerals as I was too ashamed for having lost contact with them.

Chapter 9:

My Father's House

My Dad has always had the biggest heart of any man I have ever known. He will give you the shirt off his back if you needed it. When my brother and I moved to live with him, he already had a full house and then some. With my Dad and his new wife and also stepdaughter, my Aunt was also living there, as well as one of his employees (this was a young man who needed some help getting on his feet). There was also from my Dad's first marriage, his former brother-in-law and his wife, plus their three boys. This brings the grand total of residents in this house to twelve. In a four-bedroom home. Basically, we were packed.

My Dad always loved helping people and the best way he could (short of giving money) was to provide a place to stay to get on their feet. The house was full, but it wouldn't stay that way forever. In the next months, his former brother-in-law and his family would move out and buy a home of their own. My Aunt would marry, then her and my new Uncle would get an apartment, then another until finally buying a house in the north Phoenix-area. The employee would go into the Navy and we never saw him again. Finally, my step-sister is a drug addict, so there was a revolving door for her to come into the house, rob us for drug money and get thrown out only to return a few months later and start the process over.

Despite the over-loaded house, my Brother and I always felt safe. My Dad made us feel this way, protected. He didn't need a huge collection of knives or guns. Just his presence was enough to make anyone feel safe.

Chapter 10:

Winter to Spring 1992; A Phoenix Elementary School

When we got back to Phoenix, we still had a week before school started so that was enjoyable. I must admit that I was excited to be heading to a new school. I had attended the same school (except for preschool) my entire life. Now, a new school meant a new chance to make friends. I would be the new kid, but no one would know anything about me. I had no idea how wrong I was, and I was in for a shock.

You need to understand a few things here. I am six feet tall. I have been six feet tall since I was twelve. I have a build like a football player, also since I was twelve. This means that I am larger than my peers (to this day) and have an intimidating size when compared to them. In Phoenix there is a large Hispanic population. Most Hispanic males are lucky if they reach a height of five foot, five inches tall as adults. You can imagine how tall they would be at the age of twelve.

The suburb of Seattle we lived in was largely white at the time. In fact, in the years I went to school there I remember only on black person in the school. West Phoenix has a large Hispanic population. The term 'machismo', I would learn later, was the reason for what would happen to me for the next three years. Loosely translated, machismo means strong masculinity, or Alpha male. This was the culture I had moved into, a culture that expects all males to be the strongest male around. This culture would cause me to hide my feelings and creativity for years, well into adulthood, as I often was judged, picked on and even physically assaulted as a result of me doing things that wasn't culturally accepted for males to do. Nothing homosexual, but in this machismo culture that I now lived in males played sports and were always dominant in everything they did, or at least projected the dominance whenever possible. To be creative or anything deemed non-male was to risk ridicule or worse. This was backward from how I grew up in Seattle. Without a father around from seven to twelve, I had no role model as to what a man did or how a man behaved. I learned very quickly to be quiet and not attract attention to my thoughts. In fact, my writing this book took forty years because of how I grew up around this culture.

When I started my second half of sixth grade in Phoenix it seemed that everyone was welcoming, and I was humble in coming to a new school. I was so excited to meet all the potential new friends and loving teachers. This, of course, is what is usually called the honeymoon period. Around the third week of the new school is when the first incident occurred. I was walking home with my little brother when I got shoved two-handed in the back. The shove did not send me to the ground, but it was a close call and cause me to stutter-step. When I whipped around to see what was happening, I would see a very thin, Hispanic boy making fists in a defensive stance in front of me. I was confused. I had never actually been in a fight at this point and wondered why he wanted to fight me. After all I had only been there a month and didn't even know his name. Before I could figure out the answers or get my hands up to defend myself a fist would fly and connected with my nose. Blood immediately began to run down my nostrils and across my lips. Then, the tears began to flow. I didn't know what to do, so I ran. My brother grabbed my bag that I had dropped and followed me home. This first assault was just the bringing of a new, more physical type of bullying. Once word spread that I took a punch to the face and cried, I became a target. There were several kids at the school after this who would gang up on me to terrify and intimidate me. There were about six kids that were the leaders.

One of God's gifts to me was, despite what would happen at school, I would never allow this to affect my attitude or behavior at home. I would always maintain a sunny disposition around my family, and I do not think they had any clue as to what was happening to me. After all, I had gone through much to be here in Phoenix and I would be darned if anyone was going to take my happiness about being with my Dad. Most people would be greatly affected in their day-to-day lives living through terror of this nature. God's strength was given to me to place these feelings in a place that was hidden from others once I got home.

The P.E. teacher at school was the only person who seemed to notice that I was getting bullied. Others may have noticed, but he was the only one to do something about it. One day, he rounded up the six leaders of my torment. He then proceeded to bring the six of them to the baseball field and put them inside the dugout on the third base side. Then, he brought me to the open end of the dugout and told me if any of these guys try to get by me I should try to slam them into the chain link fence, or whatever else I wanted to do to them, just as long as they did not get out before they apologized for what they had been doing to me. Then, in an extremely stern voice the P.E. teacher said something like, "Any of you M.F.s wanna keep messing with him, you have to get through him. Or, you can apologize and leave him alone from now on. That's the only ways you will get out."

I would like to remind you I was bigger than any two of them together, but I was a gentle giant. When I heard this, something in me snapped and I bent my knees slightly, got my hands to the ready and prepared myself to slam any or all of them to the ground. Then, I looked at their faces. I saw the look that they must have seen in my face countless times: Fear. They knew now that the time of bullying me was over and they were either going to pay for it physically or emotionally by apologizing. One by one, each said, 'I'm sorry' to me and I let them pass. Ironically, one of these six boys would become my best friend and almost like a brother over the next few years. After this, the remainder of sixth grade was without any major incidents, but Junior High for the next two years would be another story of utter agony.

One point of highlight during sixth grade was baseball little league. My Dad put both me and my brother in the local baseball little league. I found out that I was pretty good at this game for being twelve. I mean, I wouldn't be trying out for the Yankees anytime soon (or ever), but I was good enough that I was selected to be on the All-Star team that would compete for a spot in the Little League World Series. Unfortunately, I had to turn it down because I had to go a visit my Mom in Seattle for the summer.

Chapter 11:

New Summers

Now, when I moved to Phoenix to live with my Dad, the arrangement between my Mom and Dad reversed.

Now I would fly to Seattle for eight weeks with my Mom and the rest of the year in Phoenix. I can't remember how my behavior was that first summer, but I imagine it was better than it had been the prior November. I love my Mom and deeply regret the behavior I displayed between my ages of eight and twelve. I could go into justification for my behavior, but as an adult I accept that I made those mistakes that have undoubtedly hurt my Mom and affected our relationship to this day.

The first summer was hard. Going back to Seattle to spend eight weeks with a woman I was sure hated me because of how I had treated her was going to be a challenge, at best. When my brother and I got to Seattle that first summer, Mom never acted angry. In fact, she just hugged us at the airport, and cried. A lot. I couldn't believe that this was happening, after all I had done to her to make her want to be rid of me. She was just overwhelmed and joyful that her boys had come back. I felt shame for my behavior, but never apologized to my Mom as pride would not allow for that. I hope she knows that I am sorry for the things I did and the way I behaved.

Despite my fear and memories of Seattle being the worst place for me, I was actually happy to be there. Summer in Phoenix can be unbearably hot, whereas summer in Seattle can be pleasant and peaceful. As I grew older, I learned how much I didn't hate Seattle, just the situation I found myself in growing up there. Even more, I began to miss Seattle and regretted not taking advantage of what Seattle had to offer. To this day, I miss living there and wish I could visit, but Phoenix is and continues to be home.

Chapter 12:

My Dad's Family

My Dad's life started in Missouri and fate had led him to Seattle and, later Phoenix. Now I never have gotten to know my dad's family too much as they were in Missouri and we only visited once when I was five. Don't get me wrong, I knew they existed. I knew I had a Grandpa and my Granny (who is my Dad's mother), and they split up long before I was born. Together they had two sons, my Uncle Mike and my Dad. My Uncle Mike had three daughters and one son. Outside of this, I would hear a name or two in passing and realize they were family, but without a face to put to a name it would mean nothing.

After our first full year with Dad it was decided that my brother and I should go and spend four weeks in Missouri and Oklahoma getting to know our Grandpa and Uncle. So, once again, my brother and I would fly, alone, to a strange place. There was only one major difference: this wasn't a flight to spend a summer with our Dad, this was a flight to spend weeks with virtual strangers. By virtue of shared DNA, we were family. Outside of that, at fourteen years of age I, if truth be told, had no idea who these people were. My Grandpa had remarried before I was born, as well and, from what I heard from my Mom, this woman was the living embodiment of the Wicked Witch of the (Mid)West. Needless to say, I was terrified!

We flew into Tulsa and was greeted by my Grandpa and his wife, who said we could call her Grandma Jo. This was a good start. I spent the next ten minutes looking for her broomstick and pointed hat, and was completely shocked that here skin wasn't green. Over the next week I would learn that not only was Grandma Jo the absolute sweetest elderly person, she also treated me and my brother like absolute gold. I understand that our perceptions of people depend on our interactions with them, but whatever happened between Mom and Grandma Jo I never experienced anything near that. In fact, despite my misconception before going to visit, my memories of Grandma Jo are only positive and happy.

My Grandpa was a farmer and a retired manager for a fertilizer producer in Missouri before he bought property on Grand Lake in Oklahoma. When we visited, he was a fisherman. He would show my brother and I how to catch shad (a tiny fish) and reuse them on trout lines to catch big catfish. He would show us how to kill and clean catfish for Grandma Jo to bread and fry for dinner. He would also teach us how to drive a boat so as not to wreck or flood the boat from your boat's wake. I loved being on the lake with Grandpa. Grandpa and Grandma Jo would also pass time by playing a card game called 'Canasta'. They taught both me and my brother how to play and it was lots of fun there. We would try to continue playing with my parents in Phoenix, but the magic of that game only seemed fun with Grandpa and Grandma Jo. My Grandpa passed away in 2013 and Grandma Jo in 2014, almost a year to the day later.

After two weeks with my Grandpa and Grandma Jo it was time to go to Joplin and visit with my Uncle Mike. Uncle Mike was a Vietnam War veteran and the war years had taken its toll. I am going to tell you about Uncle Mike, but I want you to realize that most of what I know is second or even third hand and before I was born. I will tell you the facts as I know them from the summer I was there.

Uncle Mike was awesome. He was a war veteran and, as far as I was concerned, a war hero. Despite the fact that he was the heaviest drinker I have ever met, he still showed me many things about manhood. He had an awesome collection of guns that you would expect from any war veteran, and he let me shoot then when I wanted to. He also owned about ten acres outside of Joplin and, to me, it was like having your own kingdom. My youngest cousin was the same age as my brother and the three of us discovered something else that boys liked to do: fireworks.

On the back side of Uncle Mike's ten acres was a creek with a bridge and if was forested beyond that. We would get a shitload of bottle rockets and each create a 'fort' (generally made from dirt mounds and logs) separate from each other and fire the bottle rockets at each other's 'fort'. We would also throw M-80 (explosives) like grenades and aim Roman Candles at each other. Of course, those bottle rocket wars were not without its casualties. Our clothes would be severely singed by the end of each battle and there was always the occasional burn to our hands, necks and arms. For me, though, this was my equivalent to a Civil War battle. After all, I was right down the road from the Battle of Carthage (MO) and this was the closest I had ever been to were the Civil War took place.

My cousin wasn't the sharpest tool in the shed at this time in his life. I can never forget how stupid a mistake he made that made us all stop firing these potentially injurious devices at each other.

The bridge in the middle of the property is where the incident took place. My brother and I were all getting our 'forts' ready for the next battle while my cousin was standing on the bridge. I said, "Hey man, what are you doing?"

My cousin didn't reply. So, I decided to shoot a rocket at him. It whizzed right by him and he ducked. Then shouted at me, "What the hell, man? I'm not ready!"

"Well, your dumb ass is just standing there. What are you doing?" I said.

"I'm thinking." He said.

"Well, we are waiting on you. Come on, you don't have the required equipment for thinking anyway, so let's go!" I yelled.

"Check this out." He said. I saw my cousin take a rocket out and hold it in his right hand. He had a lighter in his left. He holds the rocket close to the lighter and strikes it. The fuse ignites and starts to sparkle. I am curious as to what he is thinking. The fuse is about half gone and he then holds his arm straight out, so as the rocket is off the bridge and over the little creek.

"The hell you doing?" I shouted.

"Watch this!" my cousin screams. In my experience, when someone says 'Watch This' what you are about to witness is not likely to end well. As he says this, he lets the rocket go and leans over the edge of the bridge. His head is forward enough that he can see the creek and, as his head gets there the rocket he let go ignites. The rocket flies and strikes my cousin in, what looks from my vantage point, his right eye. Screaming from my cousin is what I remember next. He falls to the floor of the bridge, clutching his head with both hands. I think he has lost an eye for sure. I get to the bridge and to him as quickly as I could and shout to my brother to go get Uncle Mike. I get to my cousin and he his screaming and crying and tossing about on the bridge, left then right, then left again. I grab him by the wrists and say, "Let me see! Let me see!"

The screaming continues as I pull his hands away from his face. Oh, the screaming. Horrific. Both his eyes clenched shut and I have him by both wrists. I see tears and snot, but no blood. I say, "Calm down! I need to see where you were hit."

Blubbering, my cousin mutters, "It hurts. Help me!"

I let him go and take the bottom of my shirt to wipe his face. As I do my brother and Uncle Mike are running toward us. I stand back up and say, "I think he may be ok."

Crying, my cousin says, "What?!?"

As he says this, my brother and Uncle have reached the bridge. I say, "There is a burn mark by his eye, between it and his nose. I don't think it hit his eye."

Uncle Mike says, "Quit your crying, you big baby. Even if you lose that eye, you still got another good one."

I say, "I think he's going to be ok."

"You fuckin' idiots are done with these bottle rockets. Dumbasses got lucky, this time. Ain't gonna be no next time." Uncle Mike says.

He helps my cousin up and we all go back to the house. Uncle Mike gives my cousin some ice and tells him to go relax. Being the oldest there, he asks me what the hell happened. I give my uncle the play-by-play. He remarks at how stupid his son is and hopefully he will learn from this incident, but he doubts it. None the less, the damage was done and we were not allowed to have bottle rocket wars ever again. I am friends on Facebook with my cousin and he works for the government and has a Bachelor's degree. My Uncle passed away in 2017 and, despite somethings that happened between him and I over Grandpa's will and my inheritance, I miss him.

Chapter 13:

Phoenix Cardinals

Yes, you read that right, I said Phoenix Cardinals, not Arizona Cardinals. When I moved to Phoenix they were the Phoenix Cardinals and changing their name did not make them any less sucky. In fact, they have never actually played in Phoenix. They played in Tempe at the time and now in Glendale. I think they should change the name back to Phoenix Cardinals or Glendale Cardinals so my entire state does not have to share in the shame. Let me say this, I am a Seahawks fan. Always have been and will be. However, I tried so hard to be a Phoenix Cardinals fan. After all, they are the home team here in Phoenix. My brother is a Cardinals fan, I believe because he was too young to remember what going to see a Seahawks game was like. There is a REAL football team and REAL football culture in Seattle. When your team has a bad year, the fans do not go and start saying how they were and always have been a Cowboys or always a Raiders fan. In Phoenix around mid-October in any given year you can find many people who just two months before were claiming to be Cardinals fans now saying, "Go Cowboys!" or "Go Raiders!" and denying anything they ever said about being a Cardinals fan, more so than Peter ever denied Jesus. It is an interesting phenomenon. Being a scholar, I have studied this over the years, using a clear scientific approach and I have been able to break it down into two distinct groups as follows:

10%ers vs. 90%ers:

First, 10%ers. These are Cardinals fans. While there are exceptions to every rule, the 10%ers have somethings in common. First, the vast majority are native Arizonans, or moved here at a very young age. They are aware of the Cardinals team history, or at least have some basic knowledge of the team (outside of the current roster). The

10%er also has a grasp of the game of football, even if it is just the basics, but could range all the way to pro-level knowledge.

Now the 90%ers. These are bandwagon Cardinals fans. They claim to love the Cardinals, especially in July and August leading up to the season. They cannot stop talking about how much they love the Cardinals and will tell you all about it, at great lengths whether you want them to or not. I never forget how much they drone on and on about how being undefeated in preseason is a clear indication of the upcoming season. The 90%er likely moved here as adults or late teens. The 90%er buys copious amounts of Cardinals gear, including canopies and other useless shit. Likely, the 90%er had little understanding about the game but tends to act like they know what they are talking about when engaged. The 90ers has every little chance of having ever played football at any level, but if they did it was to hang out with the team in high school and claim to be on the team to impress others. 90%ers tend to drive big pickups and love to reverse park in a spot, just to show off that they know how to back in with their big truck. Finally, the 90%er is usually a big asshole.

What is extremely interesting about the 90%er phenomenon is that it happens between mid-October and early November. This event occurs at or around the same time that the Cardinals are mathematically eliminated from playoff contention, if not a few weeks before when the Cardinals are starting to have a losing season. The 90%er stops all of their Cardinals speeches and hides all their Cardinal gear. Then, they will break out the Cowboys or Raiders gear while saying things like "Go Cowboys" or "Go Raiders". The major difference here is that either someone from their family, or a close friend, IS actually a Cowboys or Raiders fan and they want to fit in with a winner.

Most 90%ers are not native to Arizona, although there are a few exceptions. The distinction I have noticed is in where the 90%er came from before moving to Arizona, which directly correlates to which team they claim when they drop the Cardinals. If they came from California they say, "Go Raiders!" and if they did not come from California they say, "Go Cowboys!"

If you have lived in Arizona for any given amount of time, I probably just described someone you know. If you have never lived here, I would encourage you to come and see these creatures in their natural habitat.

All that being said, I cannot imagine what it would be like to lie to everyone in your life every year like that. That Cardinals are cursed and will never win a Super Bowl until the curse is broken. Remember, friends don't let friends be Cardinals fans and later lie about it never being Cardinals fans. Call them out and make sure everyone knows they are fake fans. Take pictures, if you must, but this has to stop. Please stage interventions for all 90%ers you come into contact with.

Chapter 14:

Back to my story:

When my brother and I moved to Phoenix, my Dad was always trying to be a good dad. He would look for many opportunities for bonding with his children, whom he had missed so much of their lives until now. One opportunity was the newish N.F.L. team in town, the Phoenix Cardinals.

At the time, the Phoenix Cardinals played at A.S.U. Sun Devil's stadium. Due to the Cardinals not having their own stadium, or being new in town and not very successful, season tickets to their home games were affordable, at least to my Dad. He would get four season ticket seats. My Dad, my brother, my stepmom and myself would enjoy eight games at the stadium. I just have to say, this was awesome.

I have always had football in my blood and to see teams in the N.F.L. play on Sundays on our T.V. was always amazing. To go to the game and actually see all the sights, hear the sounds and smell the smells was the highlight of this young man's fall. The Cards weren't very good and only won four games that year. That didn't matter because the important thing was, I was getting some serious bonding time, as well as some great football time, even if the team did stink.

The next year my Dad would renew his season tickets and we would again go to eight ball games. The Cards were on the cusp of making the playoffs but came up short as they finished 8-8. Here in lies the rub: despite only winning fifty percent of their games and not making the playoffs, the Cardinals doubled their season ticket prices. This created a huge problem for my family as my Dad could no longer afford the tickets. My Sundays in the fall with my family and football would never be the same. We went back to watching on T.V. and I have had a hatred for the Cardinals over this to this day. In fact, a colleague said to me a few years back, "It seems like you would rather have the Cardinals have a losing season than the Seahawks have a winning season." This is true. I seem to rejoice in the Cardinals demise, more so than I do when the Seahawks win.

Chapter 15:

1992-1994: Junior High

Having overcame what struggles I faced in Elementary school, I would now have another chance to be the new kid again when I started 7th and 8th grade at the Junior High. Of course, unlike when I moved to Phoenix, Junior High I knew some of the kids that would go there from the Elementary.

This was another shock, as it is for most children, I imagine. Thus far in my education I had one teacher each year all day for the entire school year. Now, I would have six teachers a day for this whole year. This may be why some of those teachers were so cold. Elementary teachers have about 30 students all year. Secondary teachers have about 150 students, which is an incredible number of children to teach every day. Prior to Junior High I think my teachers loved their students. Most of the teachers I ran into at Junior High, I believe, they could have cared less about their students, with few exceptions.

To top it off, the Junior High I attended was far from my home and not within a normal walking distance. For the first time in my life, I had to take a school bus to get to and from school. Or, when he could, Dad would drop me off across the street from the school.

Let me just get this off my chest here: I hated Junior High. Seriously. Hated it. In fact, I have yet to meet anyone who enjoyed Junior High, but I absolutely hated it. To start with, everyone is between the ages of 12 and 14 which are formative years in people's lives. These years have lasting impact on to their adult lives and, good or bad, these years change the course of human development. There is so much going on in the children's lives during this period that emotions are completely out of any type of whack. These formative years have a profound impact on people's lives when they reach adulthood. For me, there was puberty and during Junior High I was first offered marijuana.

As I said, I had a new chance to be the new kid at a new school when I went to Junior High. Unfortunately, these hopes for my life would soon be dashed. You need to understand that Phoenix, in the early to mid-1990's, was not dissimilar to a war zone. Gangs were running the majority of west Phoenix and their younger members were in the schools. These young members are always trying to prove themselves and when I ran into them, I became their target. I am six feet tall and heavily built, at that time like a linebacker. On the other hand, the gang bullies are about 5-

foot-tall (with shoes on) and about a hundred ten pounds dripping wet. Their approach to a guy like me was simple: If they get beat down by me, their excuse could be that I am bigger than they are. But, if they beat me down, well, they just won a fight over a hugely bigger guy, increasing their street cred. For me, this mantra would become a living nightmare for nearly every single day for the first months of seventh grade.

The culmination of this terror happened one day in the gym during P.E. class. When the students get to the locker room everyone is supposed to change into their gym clothes. This day, the teacher says to dress out and wait in the gym for him. I, like most students, was conditioned to simply follow directions without question. After I had changed my clothes I went into the gym. I was always quick in those days, so I went out to the gym in a hurry. There were about 5 others in the class were already there. Then, three members of the 'Hollywood' gang came up behind me and surrounded me. I remember one of them saying, "Hey, white boy, can you take a punch?"

Confused I said either, "What?" or "Huh?" and before I knew what happened a fist had connected with the left side of my jaw. Then another to the right side, and a shove in my back. Then a kick to my shin. Another punch to the back of my head. This all occurred in the span of less than 20 seconds, but it seemed like an eternity. As I think back, it's a wonder how I didn't collapse to the ground. Perhaps instinct or adrenaline kept me on my feet. I managed to push my way past the one who struck the first blow and shuffled as quickly as I could back to the locker room. As I did, I passed the P.E. teacher, who continued into the gym. Asking me nothing, saying nothing but continuing with his day. I am sure that I had tears running down my face and, possibly, blood appearing in areas around my face. I rushed into the furthest stall in the restroom, locked the door, sat down and started to cry. I cried so hard I didn't hear the hurried footsteps that came into the locker room. Between my sobbing and sniffling, I heard someone say, "I think he's in there!" Oh my God, they found me and now are coming to get more hurt on me. The door to this stall begins to rattle. Then, spit begins to fly over the walls. Bastards. Who spits on someone else?

I have never felt so alone. Everyone else who was in the gym by then did or said nothing as I was getting jumped. My hero Father could not come to my rescue. Everyone I knew did nothing or had no clue. I had no one to help me and no one to save me, I only could do one thing, pray. I put my hands together and started asking God to protect me. I prayed and prayed, all while getting spit on and banging on the door. As I prayed, I heard an older voice yell, "What the hell do you punks think you are doing!?" The teacher had come back.

When I came out of the stall, the teacher had all three of these boys standing against the wall of the locker room. He said to me, "Go clean yourself up and then you and I will talk." I went to the sink and could feel the staring from the young punks who had jumped me. As I washed my face free of tears, blood and the other's spit, two security guards came into the locker room and instructed the three to go with them. The teacher then sat with me and asked me what happened. I spilled everything through even more tears. I explained what had happened that day, as well as the terror that I had been experiencing from them and a few others. I do not know what reports the teacher filed, but I never saw those three at the school, or anywhere for that matter, again. After these three were no longer at the school, I would love to tell you that things got better for me, and that would be somewhat true. However, even more damage to my self-esteem had been done and it would take years for me to regain self-confidence and self-worth.

Another discovery I made was marijuana. Around here was about the time President Clinton made the statement about "I did not inhale.", and I figured that maybe I would find acceptance by pretending to smoke weed. I was certainly on the right path with that statement. I would always find people at the school who were smoking and I was always a welcome presence in the smoke circle. While I could lie here and say I did not inhale like our former President, I would be lying and I swore I would tell all the truth with my odyssey, no matter how ugly it gets.

If I am being honest, I certainly didn't like weed. I made me feel weird and loopy. I have always had a straight head on my shoulders and my IQ id in the 140 range, but I kept up with people who were smoking so I could be a part of something and people would think I was cool. Despite this, I wanted to be an athlete and, while I understand there are some people who would say weed does not affect their performance, I certainly felt it affected mine. The last time

I stopped smoking before I reached high school and would not smoke weed again until well after graduation.

Chapter 16:

Wrestling

There were very few good experiences in Junior High, but my absolute best experience in Junior High was becoming a wrestler. When I heard the announcement about wrestling tryouts when I was in seventh grade I thought "well, that could be fun". I must tell you, if you have never experienced wrestling, that it is the toughest sport anyone can participate in. It has been said that once you have wrestled, everything else in life is easier. If you have wrestled, you already know this. Before, though, my only experience with wrestling was American Gladiators. Their style of wrestling is a style where to win a match, all you need do is physically remove your opponent from the circle. How foolish I felt when my wrestling practice partner, Omoro, who later would become my best friend, laughed the first time I thought I had won when I removed him from the circle. He laughed so hard I am certain he peed a little bit. This isn't even close to real wrestling. Wrestling toughened me up quite a bit and I was becoming less timid and, I don't want to say aggressive, but less passive, perhaps. By the time Junior High ended, I still had a long way to go with my odyssey.

When wrestling ended the next sport in Junior High is baseball. Remember, I played little league and was good enough to make the All-Star team? I believed my natural course was to try out for a spot on the Junior High team. At this time in Phoenix there was two types of youth baseball: Intramural at your home school and little leagues. There were no 'club' teams the way they exist today.

When I tried out for my Junior High team would be my first run-in with institutional racism. There was a cultural contrivance in this district which today would be described as reverse racism. I tried out for the team and I got cut from the Junior High baseball team. While I was good enough to make an All-Star team at the little league I played at twelve years old (twelve players out of the 120 some odd players make the All-Stars), I wasn't good enough to make this coach's team out of the twenty that tried out. I don't want to go into too many details as to the quality and quantity of the racist's view because he doesn't deserve acknowledgement or power over me, but his decision to cut me based on my skin's color and not skill level created a new anger in me that would leave an anger in me. It filled me with self-doubt and caused me confidence issues, some of which linger to this day.

Chapter 17:

Omoro

During Elementary I told you about six young boys who had to fight me or apologize for bullying me and one of these boys would later become my absolute best friend. Omoro was about my height and slightly lighter than me in weight, so we were partners for practice as wrestlers. Omoro was African American, and wore prescription sports glasses with an adjustable head band, which made him very recognizable and distinguishable.

Omoro and I would spend the night at each other's houses and talk about our hopes and dreams. We were nearly inseparable for the rest of Junior High and most of High School. As wrestlers, Omoro and I both would place in the Junior High State Championships, both 3rd place at our respective weight classes, and would go on to wrestle in High School, still practice partners.

When all men work toward a goal together, they build a bond. Such as soldiers in war become brothers, so it was for Omoro and me. As we become better wrestlers, we also became good friends. Soon, I was walking to his house in the mornings before school and then we would go to the bus stop. We would hang out together after school, playing basketball in the parks, or in his backyard (his dad had paved part of their yard and put in a hoop), or my front yard, where my Dad had poured concrete and installed a pole and hoop. We would take the city bus to the mall to watch movies and, later, look at girls. At this point, we were both WAY too scared to talk to girls, but looking is what we could do. Of course, we would both talk a big game about how if we had just had one more minute, we would have gotten some girl's number but time didn't permit itself. Every once in a while, we would muster our courage and talk to a girl. Sometimes, we would get a girl's number and of course we would have to take a few days to build up the courage to *actually* call. Never mind that we would likely see the girl at school or at the mall after getting the number and God only knows what goes on in *her* head when she would see us. No doubt, wondering why we hadn't called yet. Eventually, we would each get girlfriends in our own time and think we were kings as we would meet up with the girls at the mall after we took the city bus to get there. We didn't realize that taking the bus and eating at McDonald's wasn't what you would normally do on a date, but it made us proud to be able to actually have girls that were interested in spending time with us.

Neither Omoro or I came from money. We never felt like we were poor, as one or both of us always had enough money to do things that were on the cheap end of entertainment. One of the things were could afford was riding the city bus to West Ridge Mall (now named Desert Sky Mall) and hanging out. If we had a little extra money we would go to the theater and see a movie. At the time, there was a 'dollar theater' where Maryvale Mall was and we loved the movie "Above The Rim"; we must have ridden the bus to that theater at least four times for that one movie. If you have never been to a dollar theater, it's kinda the low-end of movie going. This was a dollar theater, so the popcorn was stale and your shoes would stick to the floor, but we didn't care, we were just teens having fun and getting out of the house.

Another dollar theater was showing the movie "Anaconda" and we actually got my Dad to drop us off one late summer evening. We bought our tickets, got our sodas and popcorn, found some seats in the back and when the movie started, we realized we had made a terrible mistake: This version was dubbed in Spanish with English subtitles! We sat through the whole movie, laughing our asses off. Afterward, we realized we were laughing so hard that we didn't much catch the movie.

The tragedy of a friendship like this is sometimes as people grow, they grow apart. Omoro and I were like this. As we got older, we kind of grew in different directions, he in his direction and me in mine. If I had known what tragedy would befall him, I never would have allowed myself to become separate from my closest friend.

Chapter 18:

Maryvale High School

Both Omoro and I went to Maryvale High School after Junior High. We both would became members of the football team and found that our wrestling skills translated well to the football field. At this time, 'freshman initiation' for the football team was not only tradition but was encouraged by the upper classmen and coaches. In fact, while it wasn't fun it was, however, a point of pride to know that you were now a member of the football family. This initiation was like getting jumped into a gang. All the upper classmen would gather and basically beat a freshman for a minute or two. When I learned that I my initiation was coming soon, I stopped and prayed to God. This prayer was not one asking him to save me or protect me, but I asked God for courage and strength to take my initiation like a man. When I entered the locker room the afternoon of my initiation, nothing ever happened. In fact, I never had my initiation, nor did anyone else that I was aware of. I believe these initiations may have occurred in the past but had reached a point where they were more used to intimidate freshmen and keep them in line. Today, having coached several teams at several levels I can tell you I have never witnessed or heard of upperclassmen initiating freshman. In fact, when I was the head coach of a sport I would meet with my Seniors and explain that I have a zero-tolerance policy toward bullying and intimidation. Anyone who violates this policy would be dismissed from the team. From time to time I would hear about a football team doing hazing to players and, these days, involving some kind of sexual assault. I simply cannot understand this. I truly can't.

Chapter 18 B:

1994-1995 Freshman Year

Many of you know without me telling, but I will say it anyway: There is no pain in this life for a man like the pain involved with getting into football shape. Getting into a three-point stance when you are not physically used to it is an unnatural act that the body makes you pay for later, usually around 1:00 a.m. with intense cramps in the hamstring or calf muscles. These cramps would cause me to jump out of bed and straighten out as quickly as possible to try and relieve the cramp. The next morning, I would be severely sore from these cramps. It was horrible.

You use muscles to play this game you didn't know you have and quickly figure out if you made a mistake by playing. Most of my freshman year of football I thought I had made a mistake, not only because of the physical strain on my body, but also because we stunk. The thirty or so of us that survived the season all wondered if we made a mistake. After all, we only won 2 ball games that year and wondered if all the pain and suffering was worth it.

However, the expression goes 'You learn more from losing than you ever do from winning'. Personally, I learned that I hated losing and was determined to be a winner.

I cannot speak for my other brothers on my team, nor for Omoro, but quitting football was never an option for me. It was expected from the first time my Dad watched a Seahawks game with me. Football was a family tradition for us. My Dad played, my uncles played, my grandfathers may have played (I never had a chance to discuss with either of them before they passed), and my male cousins had played as well. There was never a moment when I doubted that I was going to play. In fact, there were conversations about how I was going to play in the National Football League and how I had to be dedicated enough to make it. I needed to believe it and have enough heart and I would get there. Can you imagine how detrimental it was to my self-image when I didn't make it to the N.F.L., let alone college to play football?

At the end of football season comes wrestling season. Naturally, I transitioned from football to wrestling. While you may think you are in great football shape, wrestling shape is quite different. While football requires things like three-point stance and bulking up in weight, wrestling, conversely, requires endurance and quickness. This requires running and lots of it. The fasting. So many wrestlers starve themselves to achieve and maintain their weight. While in the short-term this isn't an awful process, but I've known wrestlers who barely eat during wrestling season.

Being a freshman wrestler was all the more a struggle for me as I was no longer the main guy for my weight class. There was a Junior classman who was the Varsity wrestler and I got to sit second-chair to him. This made me angry. I asked God for guidance in my role and I believe God relayed to me to stay strong in my faith and work hard and I would be rewarded. So, I kept working hard and became the best wrestler I could be. This may have paid off in later years. All the hard work in the world did not allow me to take that Varsity spot this year and I only wrestled at the Junior Varsity level.

When wrestling ended, my football coach wanted me in the weight room to start to bulk up and skill training for the next season. I had something else in mind. The coach that had cut me from seventh grade baseball had stuck a dagger in my back that I wanted removed. I would try out for the freshman baseball team. When I made the team, I felt like the dagger had been taken out, but when they moved me from the freshman team to the Junior Varsity team as a freshman, I felt completely vindicated from this horrible man's decision to cut me. I wanted to call him and laugh in his face or go to the junior high school and tell him how wrong he was for cutting me, but I don't think that's what God would have wanted me to do. I just quietly smiled every day that I was on the baseball team.

God knew that he was wrong for what he did to me and I believed God led me on a path to redeem myself as an athlete.

Chapter 18 C:

1995-1996: Sophomore Year

During the summer between my freshman and sophomore year I worked for my Dad's company most of the summer. This was good because I was learning a trade which, unbeknownst to me at the time, would pay off after High School. Unfortunately, this job did nothing to keep me in athletic shape and by the time we returned to football before school started, I was in bad physical shape. As a result, instead of spending time getting work done for my football position, I would spend time getting into physical football condition. The pain, once again, returned.

My sophomore year of football was very similar to my freshman year. Get in shape, play games, lose games.

Again, we only won two games and it left a horrible taste in all our mouths. We hated losing. To work so hard and just take loss after loss should be demoralizing. Not so with us. We decided that we would stick together and continue being better at this great game. Almost every one of us that started our freshman year together finished our sophomore year and we all had come closer, almost like a family, and all dedicated ourselves to the success of our football team. What we learned this year from losing is that we had each other to stand together. The bond that was built by this team stands to this day, as I discovered when we recently had our twenty-year reunion.

When wrestling started it was pretty much the same as my freshman year: get into wrestling condition, wrestle Junior Varsity, life goes on. This year I discovered something else about myself that I thought was going to be a huge part of my life. I had signed up to be in the J.R.O.T.C. at Maryvale. From this I learned many of the skills that would make me the man I am today. Skills like leadership, dedication, commitment, loyalty, and honor. I would also try to take a path that I had thought would be the best and more glorious path that would make my life complete, so I applied to West Point. I had been convinced by many that I was going to get in to West Point by my senior year of high school, so much that I didn't apply to any other major colleges, which was a huge mistake on my part.

I soaked up every bit of information I could while in J.R.O.T.C. and wanted so much to dedicate my life to military service to the army. I would like to think that the leadership skills I learned in J.R.O.T.C. helped shape the man I became and remain to be to this day. While I would be extremely disappointed at not getting accepted into West Point, I do not regret my time spent in J.R.O.T.C.

When wrestling ended my sophomore year, I decided that I had vindicated myself enough from baseball my freshman year that I didn't need to play anymore. It was time to dedicate myself to my football career, so I spent the spring in the weight room with most of the guys I had been playing with the last two years.

Chapter 18 D:

1996-1997 Junior Year

Most of my team had taken to the weight room during the spring and summer before our junior year. We all took part in spring football and the skills players went to passing league, while linemen, like me, continued training in the weight room. During the prior summer the weight room was open but was optional. This summer, coach had made it mandatory o that to play on the Varsity team, players had to make it to the weight room at least four times a week during summer. Neither Omoro nor I had a driver's license or a vehicle at this point, so we would ride our bikes the 2 miles each way to the high school. This was great for us because the bike ride helped keep in us in athletic shape and the weight room increased or muscle mass. If we were lucky enough to scrounge change, we would the city bus, but those bus trips didn't happen very often for us. We also discovered a new muscle building product, Creatine.

Creatine is a chemical formula that aids in the building of muscle mass. At the time, we had to get it from a 'specialist' and Omoro and I drove to Cave Creek to get it (a drive which seemed like forever at the time as there were not many freeways in the Phoenix-area). It was the worst tasting stuff that, up until that point in my life, I had ever tasted. It only came in powder form, and we added it to a glass of warm water. Then, mix until it had dissolved. Finally, try and power it down the throat as quickly as possible to avoid taste. This was the art of futility as you would always get a nasty taste, no matter how fast you would drink it. It tasted like a warm mixture of chalk and feces, not that I know for certain what feces tastes like, but you get the idea. The stuff was bad, really bad. However, the results were good. My top bench press gained 35 pounds in a month and squats gained 80. We got stronger and were much better at the game of football consequently.

When our season started, it was a bit rocky. First, no one told us to stop taking Creatine when we started regular practices, so for the first few days of practice we got cramps. Once we got off that stuff, it was almost like a withdrawal. Our bodies had gotten used to having the Creatine mixture and, at least for me, I replaced it with soda. I think the sugar and carbonation mix helped.

This year was almost a 180 degree turn from the previous year. Our record was 6-3 going into the last game of the season and we had a shot at winning our region and making the playoffs. We just had to win our last game and another region school had to lose. God worked in our favor that Friday night and we pulled off a blowout victory. As we were celebrating in the locker room our coach came to announce that the other school had lost, and we were region champions! We would even go on to win the first-round game in the playoffs, but we were defeated in the quarter-final round and our season ended.

The night we lost and our season ended, was one of the worst feelings I ever had in my life. I was only a junior and knew I had one year in my high school career left, but the seniors who played with us just had their high school football careers come to a crushing stop. The bond that was formed this year was that of a tight knit family. With this end we lost some of our football brothers and most would never play the game ever again. Many a tear was shed on the bus ride that evening. I can remember asking God to give the seniors strength to get through this and keep their hearts strong. After all, we were champions and 'Once a Champion, Always a Champion'

A huge part of building a successful football team is creating a family atmosphere amongst the young men. Our coach spent time outside of practice to create this atmosphere. This is where young men build the brotherhood bond. One of the most well-known secrets of building a family is breaking bread. A simple meal with the coach and players accomplishes this. In fact, when you have a meal with anyone it should be like having them as family.

When wrestling started this year, I was finally ready to be the Varsity guy for the team. Omoro was too. We both had become increasingly stronger over the last year and now we were ready to wrestle at a highly competitive level. This year, however, would not be great for my wrestling hopes as I became distracted.

As we got into wrestling shape, I noticed that I had an admirer. This would eventually become my first serious girlfriend. This was unfortunate because as I became enamored with her and she with me. Eventually, I started to feel like she was being possessive and controlling of me. I decided to end the relationship after four months, because I wasn't going to be controlled by any woman. In hindsight, I think my Dad had much to do with me ending this. My Dad was my role model for what a man was supposed to be and how a man treats a woman. He had told me stories about his 'conquests' and I wanted to be the same way as my old man. I was gonna make him proud of his son be having as many conquests, if not more. If I was going to have as many or more notches on my belt, I couldn't stay with just this one woman. She had to go.

When I told her it was over, I felt terrible. She cried and cried and cried. This had an odd effect on me. Before, when I saw someone crying, I sympathized. I may have hugged them or cried with them. When I saw her crying, I started to get really angry. Not because she shouldn't be so upset when I explained how I wanted to not be with her anymore, but I felt like she should not have been so attached to me emotionally. This is my life.

In retrospect, I was a jerk. A complete jerk. This attitude would be a recurring theme in my relationships with women most of my life. Then, she gave me a knock-out punch in the form of "But, I'M PREGNANT!".

Naturally, this put me in an awkward position. My immediate thought was 'she has got to be lying'. I may have said something like, "For real?" or "Seriously?" I was shocked and cannot recall my first reaction. I needed a moment to compose my thoughts on the matter. Then, I remembered what my Dad said once: 'A man takes care of his family, no matter what'. This thought process caused me to consider the fact that when my parents split up, I did not have a male role model in my life for a number of years, so I thought it would be better to be involved with the child and mother and we reconciled.

This was going to require a lot of prayer. I'm only a junior in high school and now going to be a teenage father. There is so much uncertainty in this because, let's be honest, I was only a kid myself. Somehow, I think God saved me from this crooked road of uncertainty. Within two weeks of her pregnancy announcement she told me she had lost the baby. Whether or not she really was pregnant I do not know to this day. There were some signs that she wasn't. I never saw any morning sickness, but in fairness we didn't live together so I could have missed it. Usually, when a woman has a miscarriage, they see a doctor. This woman did not, to my knowledge. The fact of this matter is simple: One way or another, this huge, life-changing burden (or blessing if true) had been lifted. I tried to think of her as a girlfriend again, but the lingering fact in my mind was clear: She had made up the pregnancy to keep me from ending the relationship. I soon found a poor excuse and would break off the relationship, again. There were less tears this time. Unfortunately, this would ruin my idea of relationships with women for years. This was the first to break my trust in a woman, but there would be one more that would set me back during my senior year.

Again, to wind-down my junior year, we went to the weight room and trained for football. My senior year, unbeknownst to me at the time, would be a legendary season for our high school and was the last great team to come through in this school district, historically known for its athletics.

Chapter 18 E:

1997-1998: Senior Year

Before our senior year began, our coach laid the foundation to create a great team by having what he called 'Senior Sundays' at his home. This would involve a meal and a movie, followed by some type of character trait discussion. My senior class had stayed together throughout high school. We had been through two difficult and horrible seasons together. We also knew the taste of victory and were champions the previous year. Now, we had a chance to defend that title. We were aligned for a run in with greatness and we all were ready to become the next great high school football team.

God blessed our team with this coach and his family. He has three young children of his own and a wife who would cook meals for us once a month during the Senior Sundays to help us build this bond. The sacrifices he and his family made for us are immeasurable and can never be repaid. As a father and a husband now, I appreciate the fine line a coach must walk between his team and his family. It is a careful balancing act that few, special individuals can master.

We would incorporate God in what we did this season. There has been a movement going on in the United States to remove any semblance of God in public schools that had been going on since the 1960s. I do not know for certain if it is because we are inherently defiant or just faithful, or both, but we would pray as a team. We would pray before games, after games, before meals, before practice, and almost anything we would do as a team. God was truly at the center of our team's success.

For us, football was war. War is winnable if you have the resources and more desire to win then your opponent. We certainly had the resources and we knew our desire to win was greater than any opponent we would encounter. Every battle of ever Friday night would be, we felt, a fight for our very lives. We were certainly fighting for our pride and our school. We would never play dirty, but we had the hearts of panthers in us and we were determined to legitimize our team and our school as a football powerhouse.

By the time we played our archrival, Trevor Browne High School, we had already won our first three ball games by decisive margins. We were starting to get noticed by the local newspapers as well, with write-ups about several of our key players. Nothing else mattered at this point, though. We had to beat Browne, and not just beat them, but embarrass them on their home field. In our minds, at least at this point, our entire season hinged on this game.

When the game started, I don't think anyone on our team blinked for the first five minutes. When we finally did blink, we were already winning 19 to nothing. At the end of the game, we had won, soundly, by a score of 42 to 20. This was the victory we needed to vindicate all our hard work and losing seasons. We had defeated our worst enemy on their home field. Whatever came now, we knew we could overcome. Not just in football, but in our lives. We had a determination to be successful and the lessons we would learn from four years of Maryvale football would carry us through our lives.

When our regular season ended, we were ten and zero. A perfect season. As of this writing, twenty some years later, that feat has not been duplicated by any team in our school district since our season. We were good. I mean *really* good. Unfortunately, in the second round of the playoffs we ran into a private (rich kids) school. During this game we were winning 14 to 13. This private school decided to kick a field goal and, despite that almost everyone thought they had missed it, the referees watched the ball fly, looked at each other, then signaled that it was good. So, our final score was 16 to 14 and we were defeated by a private school. We all felt wronged and cheated. We were a largely diverse and minority, inner city school. They were not very minority or diverse and a private school. What sort of challenges had these guys overcome to deserve to win? They were not as good as us, but I learned that night that the best team doesn't always come out victorious.

Whatever the reason, our championship season had come to an end. I didn't know it at the time, but I would never play in a football game again after this.

After football had ended, I took a few days to quiet my mind. There was anger and frustration. I needed to refocus and recalibrate myself physically and mentally. I had picked up some golf clubs at the local swap meet and found myself getting grounded on the golf course near my high school. As my life progressed, golf would play a huge part in my leisure time for mental health. As long as you realize that you are not Tiger Woods, golf can be extremely relaxing and cathartic.

After I came to terms that my high school football career was over, wrestling was up next. Wrestling, as it turned out, was tragic for my senior year as well. As we trained. Omoro and I started to have some disagreements here and there. I didn't think it was anything that major, but we started to hang out less and less this year. I said before that, when people grow, sometimes they grow apart and I think that is what happened with Omoro and me.

The next real part of wrestling for me was when I wrestled the heavy weight at Carl Hayden High School. Up to this point I was having a perfect season and believed I could be well on my way to a state championship and the college of my choice as a wrestler. The person I was wrestling was my who I considered a good friend in Junior High. Now, we were facing each other as opponents.

As we were entering the third period and I was winning on points. Then, just at the beginning of the period I made a mistake and got pinned. This would be tragic because, even though I was winning and could have held on to win, I lost. Later, this other heavy weight would go on to win the state championship. The other tragedy of this season's wrestling was why I wasn't at the state tournament.

Around the middle of wrestling season, I met the next woman who I thought would be a long-term girlfriend or, possibly, wife for me. She and I would be very serious. We were together through the rest of my senior year of high school, despite the fact she was only a sophomore. We met in J.R.O.T.C. and had discussed how we both were going to join the military service after high school. I was a West Point candidate when we met, so that was where my career would take me. She intended to join the Navy after school. Things were good for me at this point as far as I could tell. What a shock I had coming from her. I'll get to that later.

As Omoro and I were training for our sectional tournament, Omoro would perform a throw on me. It was a simple headlock toss and it shouldn't have been a huge problem. However, I had my weight on my foot or the mat don't give when it should have or I resisted too much. In any case, my foot stayed planted and I would twist/sprain my left ankle as a result. Up to this point in my life it was the worst pain I had ever felt. I screamed and cried. I heard my ankle pop and I could not stand on it. I thought for sure that my season was over. Further, my best friend had hurt me. I know now that it wasn't on purpose, but at the time I was angry that he did this. Later, I would over hear him saying how disgusted he was with me because of how I was screaming and crying while there were girls around in the wrestling room. As far as I was concerned, that was the tipping point that changed our friendship.

It did not matter to me that he did this to me. It did not matter that my best friend hurt me and, possibly, ended my athletic career. None of that mattered to me. What hurt me the most was the way he reacted to my pain. His look of absolute disgust and anger at me while I was screaming and crying because of the pain left me hurting even worse and would leave its own scar on me.

I overheard a conversation he had with an outside party later saying something like, "I can't believe he was screaming like a bitch. There were girls in the room." That is what hurt, he was more concerned with being embarrassed by his friend's reaction to pain than the actual pain his friend was in. It was like a dagger had been jammed in my back, slowly twisted and slowly removed, followed by a salting of the fresh wound. I was hurt by my best friend worse than any physical injury could have ever been done.

I still wrestled in the sectional tournament, despite my ankle injury. I tried as hard as I could but lost and my wrestling career had ended as well. For a time, I was very angry at Omoro over this and our friendship was never the same. Even though we had been drifting apart, before the injury he was still my best friend. After that wrestling season ended, we never really hung out together again. We would see each other at school and say hi, but nothing outside of cordial courtesy and see each other at the occasional high school party.

The last time I ever saw Omoro was graduation night. After the ceremony, he was outside of the venue with, whom I can only assume, his girlfriend. We said something congratulatory to each other in regard to finishing high school, we asked each other about what after-party we were going to go to attend and that was it. I would never see him again.

Summary of High School

High School when I was a Freshman seemed like it was going to be an eternity. I had a conversation with Omoro during Spring of our Freshman year about this. I would say, "You know, if we are going to be serious about football we are basically going to be living here at the school for the next three years."

"Why do you think that?" Omoro asked.

I replied, "Think about it. We are going to be here every day until 9 or 10 at night during football. During wrestling we will be here until 8 or 9 at night. Then there's spring football followed by summer workout sessions."

"Ya, that's a lot of time here. You down?"

"Hell ya, we gotta be the best." I said.

And that is how we determined that Maryvale would be our home for the next few years. We basically only went home to sleep and, occasionally eat. In retrospect, those four years went by so fast and now, at age 40, seem like so long ago. At the time, those years just seemed to drag on and on, but they were also some of the best of my life.

Here is a secret to getting through school academically while achieving greatness athletically: Do the work during class. If you take the work home for home work you will never get it complete on time and then, you will struggle to keep up. Eventually you will be failing and find yourself academically ineligible to compete. This is a mistake I have noticed most athletes make today. Most of my teachers always gave the class assignments at the beginning of class and would teach to the work. If you complete the work while they are teaching, you will not have much homework, if any at all. And just to be fair on this statement, I took honors and dual enrollment, when available. For anyone reading this who was born after 1990, we didn't have cell phones to take pictures of others' work and cheat that way. We had to be creative and work at getting good grades.

Chapter 19:

Getting Carded

I turned 18 in August of 1997. Believe it or not, I had been buying alcohol from a liquor store for years and never been carded, not once. I guess I have an older-looking face. In fact, my Dad would often tell me, "Someday you will actually be as old as you look."

Nice. This also helped with my popularity as I had no problems getting alcohol in high school for parties. Then, on my 18th birthday I decided I wanted to know what it was like to get carded. I will tell you, in west Phoenix it is harder than you think and quite an overrated experience.

I wasn't going to go to my liquor store because that would be plain stupid. After all the guy had been selling my booze and beer for years and, on the off chance he cards me, I would lose future opportunity to buy alcohol during my Senior year. I first went to a 7-Eleven. I asked the clerk for a pack of Marlboro Lights. He reaches up and sets a new pack of smokes on the counter, rings up and says it's around $3. I asked him if he would like to see my ID and he tells me that's not necessary. Dammit. Never mind and I leave without getting carded or smokes.

Down the road was an AM-PM store so that's the next stop. I go in and ask the clerk, "Can I get a pack of Marlboro Lights, please?"

"Do you have any ID?"

Success! I showed the man my ID, and he replies, "I can't sell you any cigarettes."

"What? Why the hell not?" I snapped.

"Today is your birthday, come back tomorrow when you are 18." he replies.

This mother fucker. I was completely dumb-founded so I grabbed my ID back and gave him the middle finger and I walked out the door. Who the hell did the piece of shit asshole store clerk think he was to deny me smokes on my birthday? Now, regardless of anyone telling me 'they are bad for your health' or 'I don't need to see your ID' or whatever else someone says about smoking, I am on a fucking mission to buy cigs. I am now 18 and an adult and who is gonna stop me? Convenience store clerks, apparently.

I drive to the next store about a mile away, a Circle K. Same thing happens, I walk up to the counter, ask for my pack of Marlboro Lights, "Do you have ID?" I am asked, again.

I whip out my card, again, and hand it over, again. A moment passes, then, "Happy Birthday."

"Thanks" I say as the clerk reaches up and sets the pack of smokes down, while handing me my ID back with the other hand.

"I tell you what." The middle age man says as he rings up the register, "This is my birthday present to you. Happy Birthday." He then reaches into his tip jar, grabs a few ones and puts them in the register drawer. "Need matches?"

"Sure, thanks." I said with a slight smirk on my face. "You know, this is my third stop to try to get smokes?"

"Why third?" he asked. I proceed to tell him the story. "That's bullshit. You *ARE* 18 today, not tomorrow. What the hell is that all about?"

"I don't know." I replied. "Thanks, again."

With that, I got carded and it was not nearly the experience I had expected. I did get a story out of it though. This would start me smoking cigarettes for the next ten years, though, as my brain rationalized that because I was gifted these smokes, I had a duty to smoke them. After the first pack and seeing my diminished performance during practice, I would quit. I would start again, when my high school and collegiate athletics career had ended. It was around October of 1998 when I started smoking again, full time, for ten years. Sometime two packs a day. When my drinking habit got incorporated with smoking it could be a three-pack day.

Chapter 20:

1998, The First Shot at College

The only college I had applied to was West Point. I would learn by April of my Senior year that this was a mistake. During that April (of my senior year of high school) I received a letter from admissions at West Point stating that I had not been accepted, but was encouraged to re-apply next year. I also received an offer for scholarship from the University of Nebraska, but since I never applied for admission, the offer was rescinded. The only school that was interested in me at that point was Phoenix College, a junior college with a football team. I knew I still wanted to play football and needed to go to college to do so, so I signed with them on a football scholarship. I also graduated in the top 5% of my class, which got me a $1,000 scholarship at Arizona State University. I knew I wanted a military career as an officer, so I used my $1,000 to enroll in the Senior R.O.T.C. as A.S.U., while attending the bulk of my classes at Phoenix College. I kept a hold of the hope, for a while, that West Point would still be an option or, at least through S.R.O.T.C. that a military career as an officer would still happen.

Within a month of me not getting into West Point, my girlfriend told me she wanted to break up. This was confusing to me because I had done nothing to cause her to do this, as far as I knew. I told her that it was fine. I knew it would have been difficult to maintain a relationship with someone who still had two years of school to go, so I accepted her decision. Later, I came to believe she was doing this because, in her mind, I had not really gone forward with going into the military at that point and that was the life she wanted. Despite the fact that I was hurting from my friendship with Omoro ending and not getting into the college of my choice, she decided to rip my heart out. I found out months later, she was hooking up with someone else and *they* were getting serious. Again, trust with a woman had been broken and I started to think that I wasn't ever meant to get serious with woman, but just use them for my needs and discard.

This summer I started working out with the Phoenix College football team and, I have to be honest, I did not like it. Phoenix College recruited from a school, which I will choose to not name, but they were horrible at football. A big part of a football program's success is self-sacrifice at the high school level. You have to put the good of the team ahead of your own self-interests, come what may. The team where the majority of the Phoenix College recruits came from did not have this mentality and I was used to being around winners who give their all for the greater good. These people from this school were not winners. I looked around after the second week of practicing, seeing all their faces and thinking, "What the hell am I doing around these clowns". I quit football, a decision I regretted for years. I didn't know it at the time, but that would be the last time I would ever be around a football team as a player.

I was still enrolled at A.S.U. for R.O.T.C, and had my classes at Phoenix College paid for, so I decided I would continue with education. At the time, I didn't really know that there was a 5 a.m. or what it looked like. When I found out that the R.O.T.C. class meets at that time that was out, too. Not that I didn't realize what was what for a military career and not so much because of the time the class started, but getting there by 5 a.m. was the real challenge. I lived on the west side of Phoenix and Tempe was at least a 30-minute drive for me. To get up and ready on time I would have to leave my house by 4:30 a.m. This would prove to be too much of a challenge for me. Then, around September I started to realize I had no money to put in my gas tank to get me from home to classes at Phoenix

College. The pinnacle of this was when my truck ran out of gas on the way home from Phoenix College. I felt I had no other choice, so I dropped out. Well, dropped out makes it sound like I made some decision here. In reality, I just stopped going. This was October 1998.

When I realized all the crap I had been through over the last seven months and how my life had taken a turn I just went and hung it all up. I mean, I went from having a possible career playing football and potential career as an officer in the military, having a girlfriend whom I thought loved me and the sky was the limit to having no friend, no career or college, and no girlfriend. The truck running out of gas was the perfect metaphor for where I was at in my life. *I* was out of gas, having been running toward something my entire life only to fall short of goals and have nothing to show for it.

My Dad figured out that I had dropped out of college within a month. He started to talk to me about it at one of my brother's football games. His statement to me was completely out of the blue and caught me of guard when he said, "I think you dropped out of college."

Shit. "Dad, why do you think that?" I asked.

"Come on. Be honest. You never leave for class anymore. I never see you working on any college work. You never talk about how classes were going. So, yea, I think you dropped out of college."

I, of course, had dropped out and there was no fooling my Dad. "Yes, um, you're right, I just quit going. It got too hard and I wasn't feeling it." I said.

Then he asked me about my plans, to which I had none. He tells me he's going to give me a job with his company as a cable technician, since I had been working for him all these summers and have some experience. This made plenty of sense to me because I had worked for him in the summers for as long as I could remember. I went to work for my dad, which gave me a skill set in the construction industry. This would become important as I would get older because I had dropped out of college, I had no education and no skills, but now I would learn a trade. To fast forward a little bit, when the recession hit in 2008 and I got laid off while working at a different company in 2010, I was making $27.00 an hour, which was very good income for someone without a college education.

After the first semester when I had dropped out, I really believed I need to go back to college. So, making the kind of money I was at the time, I paid for my next semester of classes out of my own pocket. I had lost my scholarships, but in the back of my mind I knew I needed to go back to school, even then at age 19. Unfortunately, I would only be able to pass one of my four classes. This would lead me to drop out of college again and not return for 10 years.

There's nobody to blame for this but myself. Although, there was no one around telling me that I was too smart to not go to college, anymore, and that may have changed my odyssey. The people who said these things about 'how smart' when I was a little boy were no longer saying these things. It was as if everyone who had faith in me stopped at some point. I think the point was when I did not get into West Point that my opportunity to change the world and make the family proud was where everyone started giving up on me.

As a matter of fact, no one was giving any encouragement for me to return to school. What I was encouraged to do was to get a job, which my Dad was all too quick to offer. Basically, he had a discussion with me about dropping out of college during one of my brother's football games. That was my interview. I was told since I decided to drop out that I would go to work for him, and he would pay me eight dollars an hour (minimum wage was

$4.25 at the time). I was nineteen, a college dropout, a failure in the eyes of all who had believed in me, and now an employee of my Dad's. This was exactly where I did not want to find myself after high school.

Chapter 21:

Jacori

Another football brother was named Jacori. Jacori was probably the best of all of us. Intelligent, athletically gifted by God and basically one of the finest humans I have ever had the pleasure to meet. Jacori had an animated personality and would often be the one to light up a room. Jacori was also on the student government/council, although I cannot recall as to what position. I never met anyone who did not like Jacori, nor heard anyone say an unkind word about him. He was just that type of guy that everyone liked.

When we graduated high school, Jacori accepted a full scholarship to play football at the Idaho State University in Pocatello, Idaho. I had heard that, as a college freshman, Jacori had set a school record for returning a punt for 108 yards for touchdown, a record that will likely never be broken. I believe Jacori would have and could have played football professionally.

Unfortunately, Jacori's life was tragically cut short. Spring Break of '99 Jacori and some friends were driving home. I only know a few scattered details, but someone fell asleep at the wheel near Page, AZ and their car sideswiped a semi-truck. I received word of this the day after the accident. Jacori's funeral was held in the gym at Maryvale High School, attended by virtually hundreds of people.

With Jacori's loss I started to feel like maybe God wasn't just punishing me, but punishing those around me. Two years, almost to the day, another tragedy would befall my football brothers, an old and longtime friend, and I would end my personal relationship with God for a long, long time.

Chapter 22:

Omoro's Final Goodbye

Three years after graduation and almost exactly two years after Jacori, I would receive a phone call while I was at work. Ironically, I was at a church in Scottsdale doing some work when one of my brothers from my football team called me to tell me that Omoro had put a gun to his head the previous evening and pulled the trigger. He was at the hospital that morning and his parents were going to take him off life support, and he had died shortly after that.

So many emotions went through my head. Most of these emotions I buried somewhere deep inside or at the bottom of a bottle over the next years. I had lost my friend and I had not spoken to him in three years. God only knows what he had been going through and what brought him to a place where he felt so alone that his only choice was to take his own life. What I knew for sure I had lost the best friend I ever had for the second time, but this time there was no reconciliation, and now there never could be.

It would be years before I would deal with my feelings of losing him. I was so lost that I did not even go to his funeral, making up some excuse because I had already made plans the day of the funeral to be out of town. I think I told someone about how he had picked a bad day to die. This has been a huge burden I have carried with me since his death and only recently started to deal with. In fact, my son asks me from time to time about my best friend and why he never got to meet him. I told him that he died before he was born. Of course, my son asks, "How did he die?" to which I reply, "I will tell you when you're an adult."

Between Omoro's and Jacori's deaths, I stopped having faith and blamed God for all the bad that had continue to occur in my life. I took account all the bad: My parent's divorce, my rebellion, being bullied, being molested twice by two different people in two different states, not getting into West Point, not getting into college for football, the betrayals by the women in my life, Jacori's death, Omoro's suicide. I took all this loss and when I added it up, I concluded what I believed was an inescapable truth: God hates me. With this conclusion I told God "how could he do this? Why would he do this?" Then I said the most unfortunate thing I could, "I hate you. I will never speak to you again for this." I chose to cut myself off from the divine, and later determined to an even worse conclusion: Either God never existed, or God is dead.

Chapter 23:

Terror

Most people can recall tragic, heart-wrenching events with crystal clarity. Most people can tell exactly where they were and what they were doing when they heard the news that Japan had attacked Pearl Harbor. My Dad would tell me about when he was in the sixth grade and the principal of his school came into the room, with tears in his eyes, saying that President Kennedy had been shot. For me, I remember almost every detail the day of September 11, 2001.

In early 2001 I had moved back into my Dad's house from my apartment I shared with two roommates. Both of whom left on bad terms with me and abandoned me to a three bedroom I could not afford by myself. When this happened, my Dad offered to let me rent out a room for $400 a month. While this was not my first choice of living situations, I could not deny myself the opportunity to try and save money. Like most at their early 20s, I had little to no financial discipline, so I never saved a penny. After all, I was still working for my dad and it did make it a bit easier to live where I worked, or at least where the office was.

Although, this would come to haunt me. Dad liked to discuss business at all hours of the day and living where your boss lives means that you are never really off the clock.

I had stayed up late the evening of September 10th as I did not have to be at work until around 10 a.m. the next day, so I was planning to sleep in. Around 6 o'clock in the morning I heard a loud banging on my bedroom door. I hear my Dad say, "Wake up, the World Trade Center has been attacked.".

When I heard these words my first thought was, "Again?" Many younger people do not know, and some people probably don't remember, in 1993 a terrorist detonated a bomb in the parking garage of the World Trade Center, killing several people. When I finally pulled myself out from my bed and walked to the living room, my Dad was sitting there with a cup of coffee, alone on his couch and his eyes glued to the television. The news channel he was watching (probably Fox News) was showing the second plane hit the second tower and burst into flames, repeatedly and that was when I took full inventory as to what was happening. I went to the kitchen to pour myself a cup of joe, returned to the living room and sat on the opposite end of the couch as my Dad and we sat there for many minutes in disbelief of what we were witnessing. About the time they announced that a plane had slammed into the Pentagon, my brother had woken up and joined us. Then I decided it was time for a smoke. I refilled my cup and went to the backyard, lit my cig and too a long drag. My brother came behind me. "This is crazy' he said.

"This is our generation's Pearl Harbor." I said as I exhaled a puff of smoke.

"Yea. This is war." My brother said as he lit his own cigarette.

"At least it is gonna be. But with who, ya know? Who did this? Who is left to fight? Cold War's over. We do not have any REAL enemies left." I replied.

We sat there for a minute or two, smoking and pondering. Then, things went from bad to worse when Dad opened the sliding door, "You boys need to come back in here, it looks like one of the towers just collapsed.".

We returned to the living room and sat there the remainder of the day, in complete disbelief and awe at what we were witnessing. Watching the news reports and horror that was befalling the United States. I knew one thing that was now inescapable: the world that we had been living in was going to be changed, forever. The footage on TV that day and the replaying of the planes and then the towers collapsing still gives me a tear or two thinking about it.

The one thing that forever resonates with me, after the horror of the day gave way to night, was the silence outside. Our house was in a western flight path from Sky Harbor Airport. At any given time, day or night, you could hear a plane flying overhead. Not that night. We would often hear police sirens or hear gunshots and the 'ghetto bird' (gang violence was common in my neighborhood). Not that night. Being that it was a Tuesday, we would all be in bed asleep around 10:00 p.m. Not that night.

The silence. The silence. The silence.

Chapter 24:

Star Wars

It is no coincidence that, being born in 1979, Star Wars was and continues to be an important part of my entertainment-life. The first one I remember seeing in theaters was Return of the Jedi and it wasn't long after that these movies would be available on VHS cassette. When we got older, it would become a tradition for my Dad, my brother and I to watch the three original movies one weekend over the summer during our visits to Phoenix.

While my parents bought me 80s toys like He-Man, I always wanted the Star Wars toys. I have a cousin whose parents did buy him those toys, but he never played with them. They were kept in the original packaging and stored in plastic containers. At the time, I did not understand why he wouldn't allow me to play, but I get it now as they probably put his son through college.

For a long time the original movies were all the world got (we are not going to acknowledge The Ewok Adventures or that 'Holiday Special'), and I was reasonably enamored with the story. When we got video games to play at home or when we would get to play at an arcade the first games I would want would be anything Star Wars. Years would pass with no new Star Wars movies. Of course, there were all these urban legends that I would hear: "George Lucas is waiting for technologic advances to make more", "Never going to happen because George Lucas left the planet", but my personal favorite was "There are nine total movies that George Lucas wrote and he is going to eventually make them, once enough time passes. That's why Star Wars is called Episode 4". Turns out these urban legends were somewhat true, except for Lucas being an alien.

When Jurassic Park was released technology for computer generated images (CGI) had made a giant leap. I read an article that (I am paraphrasing here) when Lucas saw Jurassic Park he said to someone, "Let's get started on Episode 1".

I don't care what any asshole has to say about Episode 1 or 2. They were the first Star Wars movies in 20-some years and I loved every second of them. When they were in theaters, my friends and I had to see them 5 times, each. We would come home and grab broomsticks and have lightsaber battles in my driveway (yes, we were around 20 at the time).

Then there was Episode 3. I will NEVER forget Episode 3. About three months before Episode 3's release I had broken a molar on the left side of my mouth. Most people would go to the dentist right away, but I am not most people. It was bad. So bad that I would get food stuck in the break area and use a toothpick to dig the food out. I didn't realize this, but when I was doing that I was actually causing more damage. It was bad, but I had no insurance and no idea what to do about it, so I just dealt with it.

When Episode 3 came to theaters, I was one of the first in line to go. I went in the daytime so as to avoid the large crowds. About the time that Obi-Won is fighting General Grievous is when a popcorn kernel snuck its way into my hand and then my mouth. I was chewing along, enjoying the fight when, CRUNCH! It was the most God-awful pain. I was sure I had broken my tooth the rest of the way. I quickly spit everything I would from my mouth on the floor and put my finger in, along the tooth. I didn't feel any new damage, but the pain of it was far too intense. I didn't notice but I had tears running down my cheeks. I grabbed a napkin and stuck it on the tooth, for pressure. Waited a few seconds and removed. No blood. If you have never broken a tooth, you are blessed. If you have, you know the excruciating pain I was in. I did not stay for the ending of Episode 3, but left immediately and went to Walgreens.

At Walgreens I went straight to the Pharmacy. I young woman in a lab coat comes over and says, "Can I help you?'

"What do you have for tooth pain?" I asked with my left hand firmly placed on my face near where the pain was.

She points to the shelves behind me and answers, "There is a kit with some topical stuff that will ease the pain, temporarily. You probably need to see a dentist, from the looks of you."

"Thanks" and I turn to get the kit. I go to the front counter with the kit, pay and go to my car. I open the kit to find a few cotton pellets, antibacterial gel and this stuff in a tiny brown bottle. I opened the little bottle to find that what was inside smells like a dirty diaper. My first thought was anything this stinky has to work. I dabbed some on my right index finger and rubbed all over the tooth. It tasted worse than it smelled, but it did alleviate the pain in my mouth.

I would repeat the pain relief process for two days before I saw a commercial for a dental clinic that does not need insurance. I called and scheduled an appointment for the next day. When I got to the clinic I was still in a good amount of pain. Not as bad as the initial, but still hurting. It is truly amazing how our bodies can adapt to pain, when we need to. After a brief wait, I was taken back to the dentist's chair and, told I would be seen shortly. This meant more waiting. When the dentist finally arrives, he says, "How are we doing?"

What a prick. He knew by the look in my face how I was doing. "Oh, pretty good, Doc. How are you?"

"Not bad. Ok, lets take a look and see what the problem is. Open wide for me" and, at this my chair goes into a fully reclined position. After a minute I am asked, "So this is the tooth that is bothering you?" with a tap from his tool near the breakage.

"Mmm, yup." I groaned.

"Alright." the dentist says as he raises my chair back to a normal position. "You have two options with this, one we can pull it or, two we do a root canal and crown. Its up to you and what you can afford. The nurse will give you pricing options."

I said with lips half clenched, "Is there anything you can do for me today? I am in an awful amount of pain."

He nods, looks at the nurse and says, "Pack some gauze around it for now." Then, he left. The nurse looks at me, grabs a little ball of gauze, pours some fluid on it and tells me to open wide. She packs this garbage-tasting shit around not only my broken molar, but the entire left side of my cheek. It did numb the pain, for a while.

The nurse comes back with a sheet and says, "The price for extraction is $400. If you want to keep your tooth we will do a root canal and crown. That comes to $1,600. Which do you think you would want to do?"

"I can't really afford that."

"Oh, we have financing options, if you qualify." The nurse replied.

I had them run my credit and it seemed I could afford both. "I will go with the extraction" I said.

"Actually, because the extraction is so low in price, that will have to be paid in full. If you prefer to finance the root canal and crown, it will be $400 down and $100 a month."

Mother Fucker. Either way I have to come up with $400 just to get this done. "I do not get paid until a week from Friday."

"Ok, I have an appointment on that Friday at 11:00 a.m. Shall I schedule you for then?" She asked.

"Wait, I have to wait over a week to get this done? What about the pain I am in? Am I just supposed to deal with this until then?"

The nurse looked confused. "Well, if you have the $400 now I can get you in today."

Bitch. Don't you know that if I had $400 right now we wouldn't be having this conversation. "Well, I don't think I will have $400 until next Friday, so go ahead and schedule me for then."

"Alright, you are all set for Friday next week at 11:00 a.m. The doctor also wrote this prescription for your pain."

I asked, "What is it?"

"Vicodin" she said.

I need to tell you that I had never taken anything stronger than aspirin for pain, until I took my first Vicodin. I've got to say, I am a big fan of this shit. I took the prescription to a pharmacy and they filled it within 20 minutes. I read the warnings on the bottle about driving under the influence and mixing with alcohol, so no drinking for a week. I can do that, right?

Vicodin is an opiate. This means that too much can get you high and way too much can be fatal. When I got home I changed into comfortable clothes, went to the restroom and took the gauze out of my mouth, took my first Vicodin, then put fresh gauze back in. Before I could make it to my bedroom to lay down and rest I could feel the Vicodin kicking in. My legs began to feel like cooked spaghetti as I walked. I passed a mirror and saw the weirdest thing on my face, a smile. I hadn't smiled since I bit that damn popcorn kernel. Now, in the mirror I looked like the Joker. Then, I could actually see myself watching myself smile and I turned and said, "What the fuck are you looking at?'

I replied to me, "I was just wondering that myself. Shouldn't you be getting into bed, dumbass?"

Very slurred, "You're not the boss of me. Maybe you are and maybe you're not, I don't know. Stop telling me to do shit."

That was the last memory of that Vicodin trip I had. I would wake up sometime around 9:00 p.m. on the floor in front of the mirror. To this day, I do not know if I fell or laid down to get there, but I had no pain from a fall. I would later discover that I was supposed to eat something before taking the pill and an empty stomach can increase the affects.

The next week was filled with Vicodin and pain. I had developed an abscess on the outside gum area of the broken tooth and it made matters much worse as far as pain goes. At one point I swear I looked just like Marlon Brando in The Godfather, at least one side of my face. The abscess had grown so big that my left side of my face was protruding.

On the Wednesday before my dentist's appointment I had spoke with my Mom about what has happening with my tooth. She was concerned that the extraction was a drastic step and I should reconsider as losing teeth can lead to heart problem later in life. I also ran out of Vicodin on that same day.

This Thursday night was probably the worst night of my life. No pain killing Vicodin, booze was not an option. Aspirin didn't do shit because I had become used to Vicodin. I had enough at around 1:30 in the morning that night. I went to the tool box and got a vice grip plyer. I took it into the restroom and looked at myself in the mirror. I was trying to build up the courage to yank this tooth out my own self. I started to open my mouth and looked inside. Yup, the broken tooth was still there, throbbing. I also could see the abscess sack. I pushed it with my index finger and it felt somewhere between soft and squishy. Then I had an epiphany. *What if I popped and drained it?*

Holy Shit! Why didn't this occur to me sooner? I went and grabbed a push pin from the tool chest. Lit my lighter and heated the needle up to sterilize. Went back to the bathroom and slowly pushed it into the ball. No pain from the needle. That's a first. I pushed the needle almost as far in as it would go before I felt it, then when I pulled it back out, the most disgusting colored pus is slowly exiting the tiny hole. I treated it like a pimple from here on out and squeezed with my index and middle fingers as this greyish green fluid starts to pour out. As I squeezed, the side of my mouth filled with this pus that tasted putrid, as I am describing it here I can almost taste the filth again. I spit all that came out into the sink and repeated the squeezing process. Once I got to where only blood was coming out I took some Listerine and rinsed my mouth, several times. While this was gross and disgusting, when I got done I realized that I was not in nearly as much pain anymore. I had an incredible sense of accomplishment from freeing myself from the revulsion of the abscess. I was now able to lay back down and I slept through the night.

When I went to the dentist the next day I described for him what happened last night and how I almost pulled the tooth myself. He cautioned me that I should not have tried that and it was a good thing that I did not pull myself.

If I had and popped the abscess it could have killed me. He goes on to tell me that the pus could have entered my bloodstream after removing the tooth and that usually does not end well. In the end, I got the root canal and crown, paying it off $100 a month for a year.

I went back and saw Episode 3 that weekend and loved every minute of it. Today, I watch Star Wars with my kids, although not quite the family tradition it was in my youth. When we get to the part with Obi-Won and Grievous I now always check my popcorn for a stray kernel.

Chapter 25:

The Downward Spiral

The decision to close my heart from God changed everything for me. No longer would I be bound by Christian morals and righteousness. While I knew I was wrong for this I would not allow myself to feel anymore. I felt dead inside. I had been through so much in my life that I became full of hate. The kind-hearted boy was dead and now I stood as a hateful and often drunk man.

I was well past my twenty-first birthday at this time and would find myself making any and every excuse to get into alcoholic drink. And the women. There was a new one almost as often as a bus would pass through a busy intersection. I may have become a womanizer but that one is for different minds. As far as I was concerned, women where around for physical use and nothing more. An object to satisfy a hole in me that could only be filled a few moments at a time and then emptied again. They were like rubber gloves, use once and dispose. And I did. Anything you can think of that would qualify as bad; I did. I had no empathy any longer for anyone or anything. Whatever I did and how I lived my life was going to be for me now, I did not care what the consequences may be.

You must understand, when you free yourself from Christian ethics, morals, and responsibilities you are then free to do whatever you want, which is usually a very bad thing. Living life without God is like trying to live without food. You can do it for a while, but eventually you starve. The absence of the divine presence in life can be suffocating. In hindsight, God had not abandoned me, but I tried to abandon him, hence the drinking and whoring. I would do almost anything to hide the pain of not having God in my life.

Without God, things can get out of control quickly. I was smoking two packs of cigarettes (at least) a day, drinking on only the days that ended in the letter 'Y', sleeping with any woman who would sleep with me and gambling with all the money I would earn (and my life multiple times, too). Things were so bad in 2004 that, if I am being perfectly honest, I have very few memories of the entire year. The ones I do have are horribly painful to recall. My life was simply spiraling out of all control and nothing, it seemed was good to me.

Chapter 26:

One Last Chance

In the midst of this downward spiral, on August 16th, 2002 I was at a bar and, looking back, I think God tried to send me an angel. I remember it was a Friday. I was at this bar because they had karaoke and it was the anniversary of Elvis's death (any reason to drink was a good reason). I had gotten up from my bar stool and walked to the front door where the cigarette machine was. As I was bending down to buy my pack of cigarettes, I noticed a woman who just walked in. She was beautiful and looked to be just my type, and walked right passed me. When I grabbed my pack of smokes I turned around and walked to the other side of the bar where, that beautiful woman had just sat in my seat? I couldn't believe my luck, this was my in with this beautiful woman who had sat in my chair. When I walked over, I said something like, "Excuse me, but you are sitting in my seat." To which was replied, "Oh, sorry, no one was sitting here. I'll move."

Of course, I said, "No, no, no. That's alright. If you don't mind, I'll just stand next to you." This was next to the waitress's station.

She replied, "Ah, Ok. Sure.".

While I stood there, I struck up conversation with this woman over the next hour. While I do not recall all the intimate details of this discussion, I was able to get that she did not have a boyfriend and had two children. I was also able to charm her out of her phone number. This meeting would have a lasting effect on me for the remainder of my life. Our conversation would end as oddly as it began.

After about an hour standing there, talking about everything that perfect strangers could, I excused myself to the restroom. When I came back, the signs that someone had been sitting in the barstool on longer existed. There was no one there, no empty drink, no nothing. I waved to the bartender to ask if he had noticed where the woman I was speaking to went. He would say she left with the woman she came in with. This chance meeting would be a huge turning point to my odyssey's story and from here onward I will refer to her simply as "My Angel".

Chapter 27:

2004

There was one occurrence in that awful year that I am completely embarrassed about and that I have never spoke about, until now. It involves two women that I was "seeing", simultaneously. Honestly, saying 'seeing' and 'simultaneously' are the definitely the wrong words for it. What we were doing I am not sure that there are accurate enough words to describe. Let me tell you the story and you can be the judge.

I will call the first woman in this story 'Flower". Flower was a beautiful Latina woman, yet she was about ten years older than me. We met when I was 22. She had been divorced and had three kids, but the three were with their father most of the time, so she was basically single. However, she wasn't that into me, at first. When we met, she would hardly give me the time of day. She would shoot down my advances for a long time, until one evening, she succumbed to my charms and went home with me. After this encounter, she would occasionally go with me if she didn't find anything better that evening. This dynamic would lead me to tell her things like "One of these days, you are going to quit fooling around with other people who are wasting your time and realize how good I am." or "I am gonna ask you to marry me, so you better be ready when I do.". These statements would come back to haunt me, sooner than I could imagine.

The second woman in this story I will call 'Lexi'. Lexi was good looking in her way. A mixed-race woman, who was about three years older than me. We met when I was 23. Lexi was also divorced and had one child, whom she shared custody with the father. I was actually friends with Lexi's father for a long time before I actually met her. When we did meet, she was trying to set me up with her best friend. Her friend looked like my aunt, so that was never going to happen. I told Lexi this and she and I decided to hang out. Things with her were good for a time. She was really into me, which in hindsight I was afraid of. Why would anyone give a crap about someone like me? I let her fall in love with me knowing full well I wasn't capable of reciprocating. However, it was nice to have some type of female companionship during my drinking binges, which had increased to almost daily. After a time, I realized that she would practically do anything I asked.

One of the worst things I had ever done to another person occurred in the course of this story of these two women. My Dad, I believed, wasn't a very good husband to my Mom. At this point, I thought I could be a better husband to anyone than he had been to my Mom. Just a quick note here, my Dad has been a great husband to my Step-Mom as far as I can tell.

Lexi and I were lying in bed in the very early morning hours in some winter month in 2004. I was still drunk and reflecting on things that had been happening. I remember waking her up and asking her something like, "Do you think we should get married?"

Of course, her reply was, "What the hell are you talking about?"

"Yea, I think we should get married." I said.

"You're drunk, go back to sleep." Lexi replied.

I said, "Yea, I am. But I think we should get married. Thing are good, I like you, a lot. We have good times and I think we should go further. I have been thinking about it and I think we should."

At this Lexi sat up. "You're serious?"

"Yes." I really should have given this answer more thought before I spoke.

"Oh. My God, you know I am so in love with you. I was hoping you felt the same. Yes, I will marry you."

I never said 'I love you' to her. I didn't, but this is what people do when they have a good relationship, right? They get married. Of course, I made a mistake at this entire conversation. I would make a worse mistake the next morning. This was a Sunday morning.

Lexi left as the sun was rising and I went back to sleep for a while, to sleep off the remaining booze and whatever else I had left in my system. Sometime around 11 a.m. my phone would ring. At this point, I had not seen Flower in a few months, but now she was calling me with a mutual friend on a three-way call. The hazy details of the conversation elude me, but the important thing was Flower had called and asked, "Does my marriage offer still stand?"

I hesitated. Was I still drunk or high? Was I asleep or awake? Didn't I just have this conversation a few hours ago? I was panicked, so I said, "Why, what happened? What changed?"

Flower said, "Nothing. I just want to know if you still want to marry me. Cause if you do, I will say 'yes'."

I replied, "I already told you I did."

"Then go get a ring. Your answer is yes. I want to see you later tonight. I will call you later." and she hung up.

This was very confusing to me. I thought she had said 'yes' last night. Did I dream that last night? God my head is pounding. Need coffee. Then it hit me like a ton of bricks. I had just asked a second woman to marry me within 24 hours. I was now in a pickle between two women that both think I am going to marry them. Serious decisions to make and I am sure I didn't understand the gravity of what was happening. On one hand, I could choose Lexi, who was completely in love with me. On the other, Flower, who on a good day may acknowledge I exist. In reflection, I should have acted; should have done something, anything instead of what I did. Being the person I was at this time in my life I did what I did: NOTHING.

This would have been a good time to pray, but that wasn't on any agenda in my immediate future. God could have prevented these types of poor decisions from my life, or at least would have steered me in the right direction, if I had asked. My life, at this point, felt like I was totally alone, so asking God for guidance wasn't an option.

Besides, I was still angry with him for all the crap that had happened to me.

Then, I thought I should drink this over. Any good decision up to that point had been the result of alcoholic thought, right? For the briefest of moments, I went to the kitchen to make an eye-opening Bloody Mary, but when I got there I thought 'alcoholic decisions had created this situation, probably shouldn't drink to get out of it'. That process lasted as long as it took to pour and mix the Bloody Mary. Many a strong drink went over the lips and through the gums.

As I drank, I thought about life, my life. How did I get here? What had I been doing since high school with myself? Jack nothing is what. Here in lies my major problem, no matter what I do now, I cannot keep whatever integrity I have left with one or the other woman. Furthermore, we all share many of the same people as friends, so this will destroy multiple relationships in my life whatever I decide.

Then I thought about My Angel that I hadn't spoken with in a few months. What would happen if she came back into the picture again? Never mind that, can't think about the 'what if's', gotta focus on the 'what now?' factors. Already enough variables. The conclusion I reached was much to my everlasting shame. I already had Lexi, but I wanted Flower. Now I was in a position to have her, forever I thought.

My game plan was this: go get as nice a ring as I could afford for Flower, see her later tonight, and avoid Lexi at all costs, until the end of time. Foolproof.

This was Monday: I went to the mall, found the first jewelry store, had them run my credit, got approved for $1,500 credit line and got a ring for $1,200. I didn't even know her size, but I knew enough about her that as long as it was sparkly, it would be sufficient.

This was Tuesday: I called Flower and set up a dinner/date at a Mexican food place near my house. We met, I gave her the ring and off we went on what in my mind was going to be my happy life with this woman who I barely knew anything about. Those little things would come with time, anyway. I was now engaged and determined to be happy. Whatever brain I was thinking with, it wasn't in my skull.

After dinner, we decided to celebrate at the bar we met to announce to our friends what we were intending. There were several of our friends there, no Lexi and My Angel weren't there either, by the grace of God. Ironically, my Dad and step-Mom were there too. Perfect time to tell them the happy news too. My Dad's response was less than I expected. He said something like "What the FUCK are you thinking?"

My step-Mom intervened his displeasure by saying, "Dear, it is his life, if he is going to be happy, we should be happy for him. And if he is going to fuck it up it is on him, too."

"Thank you." I said.

Then God dropped the hammer on my parade. Lexi walked in the bar. My first thought was 'RUN!', as this is no time for heroics. Take the coward's way out, I thought. She quickly noticed me and I saw her give me a quick smile, but I turned around to show my yellow stripe on my back just as quick. I don't know what she did for the next few minutes as I tried to ignore the problem, but she had left within five minutes. Had she figured it out on her own what I did or did someone tell her? Just as soon as I figured out she left, one of her friends came up to me and said, "You know what? You're an asshole!"

I would say something, probably incoherently, like, "Get outta my face. You don't know anything about it. She tried to set me up with one of her friends first."

"Get the hell away from us before something happens to you." Flower would shout. Lexi's friend clicked her tongue, rolled her eyes and walked away. Then, Flower would say, "What the hell was that bitch's problem?"

"I will tell you later." I said, "Let's just try to enjoy the evening."

We stayed at the bar until closing time. Then, Flower said, "Are we going back to your place or mine tonight?"

"Let's go to yours." I said. I don't know if she knew that I was living at my Dad's house, but this was no time to bring that up. This was, at least in my head, about to be the goal of a lifetime for me. The pleasures I was hoping to experience, would be the stuff that songs were written about. Unfortunately, often what is built up as anticipation rarely is fact. The fact was that Flower passed out in my car on the way to her apartment. Getting her to the third floor would be a challenge. I am a strong man, at least I was then, but carrying a woman up three flights of stairs, who would be dead weight, could cause life-threatening pressure on my heart. The solution came to me as I was considering carry and climb. I had to wake her up.

It didn't take as much as I thought it would to wake her up. Just a couple of times saying her name loudly and a touch on the hand did the trick. When she roused, she said, "Oh, we here already? Did I pass out?"

"Yes, to both. Ready to go upstairs?" I replied.

"Yup, but could you carry me? I'm really tired."

I swear my jaw hit the floor. Was she serious? If I had known that she wanted me to carry her anyway I don't think I would have woken her. Then, relief, "Just kidding, come on." she said as she opened her door.

I opened my door and got out. This was going to be awesome. I knew little about this woman, but that was ok because she was super-hot. We started the climb up the stairs, me right behind Flower. When we made it to the landing at the entrance to her third-floor apartment she paused, turned around, looked me in the eyes and said, "Are you ready? I know you've been wanting this for a long time."

I said, "Hell yea." As I placed my hands around her hips, pulling her into me and kissing her. It lasted only the briefest of moments before she broke away, turned to unlock the door and we both would enter. When we entered, Flower began taking off her clothes in an expedited fashion all while saying, "The bathroom is there," motioning with her left hand, "I'm sure you need to go."

I did. Lots of alcohol running strong, but urinating was becoming the foremost thing on my mind, even more so than her. "Thanks." I said as I went in the direction Flower motioned. I went to the restroom, closed the door behind me, took care of the restroom business, flushed, washed my hands and face and paused at the mirror. Was this about to happen? Could the physical woman of my dreams be about to become my wife?

Strange thoughts started to swirl through my head. The room began to spin. Was I drunk? My heart began to race. Then I took a moment to think about Lexi. What she must have been going through that night. What I was about to be doing versus the pain she had to feel knowing what she now knew about my horrible decision. Dizzy. I closed my eyes. Darkness. I used the vanity to hold myself and regain composure. Get it together.

I ran the tap and splashed the cold water on my face. Alright, let's do this. I came out of the restroom and

181

went through the living room area, then to the bedroom door, half shut. I opened the door to find Flower laying on top of the sheets, naked and passed out, again. I went over to the bed and tried to wake her, again. This time, I was unable. She was pass out for the count. "Oh well." I thought. I have a lifetime now, what is one more night to wait.

This was Thursday: I went to the bar to hang out, Lexi didn't want to come telling me she wasn't up for it. I went anyway. Don't remember much but hanging out with four or five people I knew.

The hammer came down that Friday: I was on my way to a jobsite in Tucson when Flower called me. The details of our conversation are a bit hazy as I was kinda hung over, but I remember she said she was going to our bar tonight, but she didn't really want me to be there. Something about wanting to hang out with her friends, and

I should do the same or relax at home and she would call me when she was leaving. Seemed ok to me, at the time.

I returned home around five that afternoon. I took a shower and tried to relax. I poured myself a Jack and Coke and went to the backyard for a smoke. I figured I might as well have a few drinks since my fiancé was out having some, too. Around seven that night I got a call from my brother. He said, "Hey bro, got a quick question for you."

"Ok, go for it." I said back.

"You and Flower still getting married?"

Curious question. "Yes, why do you ask?" I replied.

My brother said to me, "You need to get yourself over he to the bar. You need to see this for yourself. I can't believe it and I think you need to see with your own eyes."

"Just tell me what is going on."

"Well, she is here and she ain't actin like someone about to get married." He said.

My heart just sank. I knew she couldn't be loyal, but I thought marriage might change that. "What is she doing?" I said.

"Just get in your car and drive over here."

I replied, "Dude, I'm half drunk."

"So what? When has that ever stopped you before. Come on and get here, now!"

"Alright." I hung up the phone. God help me, I thought. No, he and I ain't talking. What to do? On one hand I promised the woman I was getting ready to marry I would stay home tonight. On the other, my brother whom I trust more than anyone else in this life is basically telling me my fiancé is not acting like she should be.

What to do? If I show up and there is nothing going on, I will feel foolish and, possibly, lose what I had hoped would be a great marriage. If I trust her to do the right thing, I would not be trusting my instincts. If only I could pray and ask God for guidance. My pride, my anger and my moronic ways would not allow me to speak to God this night. I got dressed and went to the bar.

Most nights when I come to this bar I would park in the back and enter through the back door. Not this night. I parked in the front and entered through the double doors. In my mind, this was the sneaky way to observe what Flower was doing, hopefully unseen. I knew that if she spotted me, there would be all kinds of hell to pay. What I didn't know was if her behavior would end this relationship before it was started.

When I entered the front entrance of the bar I calmly and coolly, but quickly, moved from the entrance to the nearest barstool. As I moved, I saw her, plain as day, sitting at a table with her ex-boyfriend. I was crushed, for a moment. Then, anger. However, I would have a moment of clarity: I will watch her and see if it is innocent. My bartending friend come over when he saw me. "Hey man, wuz up?" he said.

"Nothing, just chillin'." I replied.

"Miller?" he asked.

"Not tonight, just a water. Kind of need to keep my wits, and I already been having a few at home."

"Cool. Flower's over there. Did you see? I told your brother to call you so you could see for yourself."

"He did. Thanks for looking out. I figured I should keep an eye for a bit to see if its innocent or what." I said.

"It ain't, I been watching, and she been doing you wrong with him since they been here."

"What does that mean?" I asked.

"I know it appears calm now, but they been holding hands, kissing and at one point I thought I saw his hand go in her shirt."

I was devastated at hearing this. I may have had tears forming in my eyes, but the anger kept them from flowing. Ultimately, I may have knew this was going to happen. After all, the saying goes, "Never try to make a whore a housewife." And I should have known better. Now, I need to decide what to do. If I make a big scene it will likely turn into a fight with her ex. In that case, he isn't a very big man and I would likely hurt him in a bad way. Especially with the fire that's in my lungs tonight. If I just leave and talk to her when I am calm, she may try to explain it away and I could be fooled. Technology has provided me my out: I will leave but send her text messages from the parking lot. I said goodbye to my bartender and quickly moved out the door. When I got into my car, I took my phone and typed the following message:

"Flower, I just left the bar and saw you with your ex. I can't believe you would do this to me. Please give my ring back to our friend that we both know, and I never want to see you again."

Then I sat for a minute or two and just thought about what I was about to do. Am I sure that this has happened? I saw some of it with my own eyes. Eyewitnesses told me more than I saw, but why would they lie. I pressed "SEND".

I decided to pull my car around to the back of the bar and wait. Then my phone annunciated. A text message, but from my brother, "Hey man. Did you come to the bar? She is still here with that dude."

I texted back: "Ya man. I was there for a minute. Saw what I needed to see. Thanks for looking out."

Another annunciation, this time from Flower: "What? Where are you? I wasn't doing nothing wrong. You should not have been spying on me. Please come back so we can talk."

I read her message several times. I think I still have bourbon coursing its way through my brain. I must focus here as this will be a life changing decision again. I texted back: "Please, I saw you with my own eyes. There is nothing left to be said. I am through with you and we are done. I hope it was worth it. Leave my ring with our friend and please do not contact me ever again." Sent this message right away this time.

The guilt of this proposed marriage to Flower started to creep into my mind. What had I done? Then I thought about how awful I had hurt Lexie over this and how she must hate me over this. What a horrible person I had become. Then, for a moment I thought of My Angel that God had sent me on one summer night in 2002. I heard another annunciation from my phone. I don't care. I pressed the power button and turned it off. I am done with this shit for tonight. Time to go home and get drunk. Really drunk. Need to take the pain away of this life for a while.

This is Saturday: When I woke up the next morning, still drunk and my heart hurting, around 11 a.m. I never have been able to stand the taste your mouth develops overnight after heavy drinking. It feels like a combination of sand and snot, somehow. After a quick trip to the restroom to pee and Listerine my sandy, snotty mouth I would wonder to the living room and turn the T.V. on. A movie was just starting on the channel that was open, "Love Stinks". God is not without a sense of irony, it seemed to me. All this happened in the course of one week.

The next week I would pick up the ring from Flower and I's mutual friend. I returned it to the jewelry store for a full credit return, as it had only been in my possession for a week. To this day, every time I pull my credit report, I have a nice reminder of that week's events as the credit line that the jewelry store opened for me is still there.

The irony of these events is that I was no wiser for the wear. I was still completely stuck in stupid mode for years to come. Over the rest of 2004 and into some of 2005 I would occasionally run into Flower, at least from what I can recall, and when I did, we would often end up at a hotel room.

I would see Lexie occasionally too, but she didn't want much to do with me after this understandably so. We would keep in touch for a while and, occasionally, have a drunk hook-up and I think she still was in love with me. After some time, she let me know that her job was moving her to another state. Honestly, I think it was to get away from me and for a fresh start.

Chapter 28:

The Blur

I refer to this time period of my life as "The Blur" because most of my memories from 2005, 2006 and 2007 are a bit of a blurry haze spent in alcoholic stupor as often as possible. I mean I was drunk as a skunk 5, 6 sometimes 7 days a week. What I can remember doing was a lot of stupid shit that could have gotten me killed or worse. These were the bad times. I remember a few close calls with drunk driving. I had bought a Mitsubishi Eclipse and thought it was the coolest thing because it was a sports car. My Dad would often refer to it as my 'pussy wagon', because he thought it would attract all kinds of women. He wasn't entirely wrong. I would wake up every Sunday afternoon and wash my car like clockwork. I really loved that car. It was like my baby.

One night, someone took a bucket of sky-blue paint and poured it on the top of my baby. I never found out who did it, but best I could figure it had to be someone I probably should not have slept with or the husband/boyfriend of someone I probably should not have slept with. After about a year of trying to get the paint off by myself, I was able to trade my baby in for a pickup truck. Not my first choice of vehicle at the time, but I did get the paint off through a dealer. This is how ignorant and foolish I was at this time: I could have turned a claim into my insurance and got a new paint job. Live and learn.

Unfortunately, I wasn't being very responsible and financially I was becoming a wreck. To support my 5 to 6 to 7 day a week habit and my pack or two of cigarettes a day I was deciding as carefully as a drug fiend would as to what bills needed paid and which could get their corners cut. My largest expense was the pickup truck, so a few payments would get missed. By May of 2007 I was 2 months behind. Coincidentally, that April I was offered an iron-workers position in Loveland, Colorado, which I accepted. Of course, I called My Angel out of the blue to tell her I was leaving Arizona and wished her all the best. This sort of rekindled a relationship, but I am getting ahead of myself here.

During the Blur, I cannot remember much relationship-wise. Excepting a few near misses that are as horrific as embarrassing to remember. One evening sticks out. I was sitting at my favorite bar having a few beers on a Friday night. This woman sat next to me and started a conversation that went something like this:

"How ya doin?" she said to me.

"I'm good. How are you?" at which point I noticed this woman's figure and face. Lord, I remember thinking to myself "Please, God, let me seal this deal". She had eyes like a doe and a face of an angel. Dirty blonde hair and built like a Greek Goddess.

"Oh, I'm much better now."

"Why is that?" I inquired. Thinking I was going to get the usual answer of its Friday night, long week, blah, blah, blah.

"Because YOU are here tonight." she replied.

Oh, my, God. Did this Double D-sporting Playboy Playmate-looking woman just say she was here for me? Oh, now I get it. She is messing with me. "You came here tonight for me, huh? How's that? You been stalking me?"

"Kinda. I love the way you sing. Your blue eyes too. Would you sing a song for me?"

"Wow. I've always wanted a stalker. Especially one that looks like you." I joked.

"Oh. Hahaha. I am serious. You sing so amazing."
she said with a half drunken smile.

"Alright, what would you want me to sing for you?"

"Anything by Elvis, your voice is so sexy when you
sing Elvis."

At this, I looked her in the eyes. Now I know she is
messing with me. This woman could barely be old enough
to buy her own drink, let alone know who Elvis was. I said,
"Girl, what you know about the King?"

"Nothing. I just love it when you sing, and your
singing makes me so hot." she replied. Is she messing with
me? Let's test these waters a little.

"So, you love my singing, huh? Tell you what. Let's
get a shot of tequila and chill until I can sing you that song.
What ya think?" My thought was if she is messing with me,
she is gonna want to stay kinda sober so she knows what
she is doing.

"I usually don't drink tequila. Bad experience. But, anything you want, I am down." she told me.

"Anything, huh? Like that?" I asked.

"ANYTHING." My God. Please don't let this be a joke. If this goes down like I think its heading I must have down something right in my life.

I ordered two shots of Jose Cuervo, we touch our glasses together, slam the drink and chase it down with a beer. Then I hear the DJ call my name. I give her a wink as I get up and grab the mic. I cannot recall what song I sang, but when I got done and returned to my seat, she practically ripped my head off with both hands as she shoved her mouth onto mine. Tongue and all. I was so stunned that this beauty was not messing with me at that point I don't know how I reacted, except to make out back with her. After what seemed like an eternity she breaks away and says, "See. I wasn't lying. Your singing makes me hot."

"No, no you weren't." I signaled the bartender to settle my tab, but not before we had another shot of tequila, each. "So, did you wanna go somewhere and have a little more drinks and privacy?"

"Yup. I'm staying with my aunt. It's not far from here. If you have your car we can go there."

"Are you sure she won't mind? I can get us a hotel or something." I replied.

"It's cool, we can just go there."

"Did you drive here?"

"No, I got dropped off by my (she trailed off). My aunt dropped me off."

"Alright." I said.

I probably should have pursued this line a bit more, but I was drunk and pretty sure I knew what I was about to get into and was not thinking with the right head.

We shuffled out to my Eclipse. I helped this beauty into the passenger seat and I went around to the driver side, got in, started up the engine and asked, "Which way is it?"

"I don't remember for sure, but I'll know as we go. Just go to the road and take a right." she tells me.

I see her starting to lean her head back out of the corner of my eye, and her mouth open in a 'I'm passing out' position. "Hey, don't pass out. I don't know where I am going or where you live. Are you sure you don't want to go to my place?"

"No!" she said in a hurry. The way she said 'no' made me think things were about to take a turn. "Just go to my aunt's house." As she said this she also mumbled something, but I couldn't quite make it out. Remember, she wasn't the only one drunk in this car as I was quite inebriated as well.

I continued down the main road for about a mile. Then, a shout, "Make a left here!"

I veered the car to the left and got in the turn lane. Waited for the light to change and then, made a left. "Ok, now what?"

"Just keep going to the park." she said. Now, I feel I need to tell you I know this area well. This park she is talking about is across the street from my high school. In a few minutes I came to a four-way stop intersection with the park across the road to the right.

"This park?" I asked.

"Yea. Just take the first right past the park."

I drive my car to the road and take the right. I pass two houses when she grabs my right forearm and shouts, "STOP!".

I slammed the brakes and stopped the car; I looked at her as she fumbled to open the door. When she finally figured out how to open the door, she tried to get out, but more rolled out, or even flopped out like a fish, to fall on her knees and crawled toward the park. She made it about ten feet before totally collapsing. Then, she begins to puke while lying flat on her stomach, arms at her sides and head slightly turned right. I put my car in park and get out, only to realize I am super fucking drunk as well. I stumble over to where she is and try to help her, but I realize that I am now too drunk to concentrate enough to lift her. As she is more or less on her stomach with her head turned now to the left, I don't think I became concerned about her drowning in it. I gathered whatever senses I could and stood over her, reached down and hooked my hands under her armpits and lifted. No luck as I was too weak from the drink.

It has always amazed me how you can be super drunk in one moment, but not a moment later you almost get clarity and sober. These sobering moments come in times of crisis or panic. I had one of these almost sober moments at this time, so I tried to help her again. I took my hands and hooked them under her armpits, again. This time I decided to slide my feet forward so as to get her out of her puke. I said, "Come on, we gotta get you out of this vomit."

She mumbled something as this woman struggled against me to leave her there. I did not have the coordination to continue moving her, so I gave up. I was able to move her about a foot away, but as she was dead weight and I had no strength left she was still basically laying in her own vomit. At least her face wasn't in it anymore. Hopefully, I thought, she is done puking or this has could go to a potentially deadly situation. How did this from having very exciting possibilities to this? I did the only thing I could think of to do: I called my brother.

He showed up in what seemed like record time. I explained what had happened and asked him what he thought we should do. There was no easy solution. He asked, "Where does she live?"

"I don't fucking know. Probably somewhere close by, I think. She was telling me how to get there when she bailed out of my car to puke." I replied.

"But, you don't know for sure?" he said.

"No. No. We never got that far."

"Dammit Man! What are we going to do about this drunk bitch? I don't think we should try to lift her. Was she with anyone at the bar?" he asked.

"Not that I can remember." At this point, I think the adrenaline of the situation took over my drunkenness and I started being a little more coordinated. "Maybe I can lift her back into the car and drive her to my place, for now."

"Don't do that. She wakes up in a strange place and she don't know you she might claim rape or some shit."

"Fuck. What then, we can't stay here all night." I said.

"*We* can't, but *she* can." He said.

I stood there, half drunk, mouth half open and completely bewildered. I replied, "You can't be fucking serious. We're just leave her drunk ass in the park?"

"Not we, you. You brought her here so whatever happens is on you. I will help, but you have to decide and do it quick. I mean, what else are we supposed to do?" he says as he starts to use his fingers to count, "You don't know where she lives, so you can't take her home. You probably don't even know her name, do you?" I shake my head, no. "Then what do you suggest?"

I did not have a suggestion. To my great shame and embarrassment, we left her there in the park. I went back in the late morning to see if she was still there. There was a stain in the grass where she had puked. I could still smell the alcohol smell from the vomit. It made my stomach hurt. I could see where the grass and dirt had been smooshed by her laying there, but she was nowhere to be found. To this day, I cannot remember her name and do not know what ever happened to her. I have never spoken of this event until now, even with my brother to see if he remembers any details. Honestly, because of how often I was drunk during these years this whole event may have been some kind of drunken nightmare, or it could have happened. Either way, I am afraid to ask my brother just in case it really happened.

Chapter 29:

Quads

There was another adrenaline rush I learned that I had a love for during The Blur: quads. A friend of mine who was an auto mechanic, Don, and he owned ten acres of land out west of Buckeye, just off the west side of the

Hassayampa riverbed, which is dry except during flash floods in monsoon season. My Dad had bought two quads from a private seller and Don graciously allowed him to park them on his land. For a few months our every free moment would be at Don's place. We also learned that we were great drunk drivers on quads as well.

There is a certain freedom that comes with driving a quad, out in the open desert. It can be an adrenaline rush to drive into the unknown and hope you don't break any bones if you crash. If you do this while drunk, the craziness can be all the more thrilling.

What you need to know about the Hassayampa riverbed is that it is well traveled, so much so that there are some very distinct paths in the sand. This is because every weekend, racers would get together there and have organized competitions. We never got involved with those, but we would have our own brand of fun.

After two or three weeks of going out to ride, I decided to take off on the larger of my Dad's two quads by myself. I was going to ride north for a way, then come back. I wasn't sure how far I would go, just knew that I was going to go. As I headed north on the riverbed I noticed there seemed to be a trail on the west part of the bed. It seemed sort of smooth and not very exciting. When I got to where I though I was far enough north I stopped and turned around. I thought, 'this ride has kind of been a bust'. Then, I saw another path, rough and dangerous, on the eastern bank of the riverbed. Here was the excitement I was seeking. I went over to the other side of the riverbed and started out south. I opened up the throttle and I quickly realized this path wasn't well developed or traveled, but I kept hauling ass south. Then it happened:

I was likely doing between 35-45 miles per hour, no seat belt, no helmet, short sleeved shirt and tennis shoes. There was a drop off, my guess was about 5 feet, but maybe 6, right in the middle of this path. It was like a cliff in the middle of the road. You know how in movies, when the star goes airborne everything seems to slow down? This happened to me. As soon as my front tired left the ground it was slow motion. I was in the air completely when I realized I was in deep shit. I remember thinking, 'this is going to hurt'. I had the sense to lock my elbows, tighten my thighs as tight as I could around the seat and then, "BOOM" and I landed. I briefly felt the backend of my quad lift, so I naturally leaned back into the seat and locked my arms so as to keep myself from flying over the handlebar. I felt my body lift from the seat and start to go forward, but only through the grace of God, I landed safely. After this, I went across the riverbed and rode back the rest of the way on the path I knew was safe.

Another weekend, Don, another man named Johnny and I decided we wanted to ride to Wickenburg and have a beer. Our plan wasn't well thought out as we just hopped on our quads with a cooler full of beer, but no water, and started riding north along the dry riverbed. The ride went well for about half the way to Wickenburg. I told the others I needed to stop for a minute to pee, but that they could continue, and I would catch up. After I finished, I decided I wanted a smoke, so I fired one up and grabbed a fresh beer from the cooler. I smoked about half my cigarette, put it out, slammed the beer and jumped back on my quad.

After I jumped back on my quad, I started out toward the north again. I opened the engine up to full throttle to catch Don and Johnny as quickly as I could. They were taking a slower pace, knowing that I would be catching up. As I approached, I could see both of their quads in the distance. I continued and then I witnessed what could have cost one or both of them their lives.

I was about 200 feet away from Don and Johnny, when Johnny jerked his quad to the left, clipping the front-end of Don's quad. This action caused two things: Don's quad flipped over, landing on Don and Johnny was thrown across the front of Don and landed in the soft riverbed. I witnessed the entire event from my distance and could not believe my eyes. Here we were, in the bottom of a dry riverbed and almost as close to the middle of nowhere you could be. No time to panic so I speed along as quickly as I could get to Don's flipped quad. I could only hear the whine of my quad's engine as I got close.

When I got about thirty feet away, the dust from the crash had cleared and I could see Johnny looking under Don's quad. I wasn't sure if Don was alive yet, but could tell Johnny was alive, at least. Then, I got close enough to see that Don was alive, but pinned beneath his quad, which was resting on his left thigh. I jumped from my quad and went to try to lift the quad from Don. As I lifted, Johnny assisted me, Don screamed, and we were successful in flipping Don's quad to the upright position. Then we saw when Don screamed: the quad had cut into his leg. While blood wasn't running out like a life-threatening wound would, this was no scratch either. I went back to my quad and grabbed a rag that had been on the back of my quad since my Dad bought it. As I started toward Don he said, "Is that sanitary?"

"Probably not. But Dude, you are bleeding and we gotta stop it." I replied.

"Not with that. I will get an infection and die from that. Grab a beer." Don said.

"I think I've had enough at this point, don't you?" I asked.

"It's not for drinking, just go get it." Don told me as he took his shirt off, wrapped it around his hand and pressed it on his leg wound. I did as I was told and grabbed a beer from the cooler, took it to Don, and handed it to him. Don opened the beer, took a big slew, then poured it directly on the wound. His face grimaced from the stinging pain. At this, Johnny threw up.

"That's so nasty!" Johnny screamed between gagging and hurling.

"Fuck you, you little asshole. This is your fault. Where did you learn how to drive like that?" Don asked.

"Ok. Let's not fall apart. Hopefully your quad will run and he can get it back to your place." I said. I was able to roll Don's quad back over. I pressed the ignition and it fired right up. "Don, can you ride?"

"What kind of question is that? I am not going to stay here and bleed to death in this God-awful desert, so I damn sure have to, don't I? Ain't no other choice."

We took our time riding back to Don's place, making stops to check his leg, which was still bleeding, but looked slowing down to me, but by the time we got to the house his leg was a bloody mess. While the gash in his leg didn't seem that large to me, the way it bled made me think perhaps he had a deeper wound, like a vein or artery cut. His wife was a nurse and got out the first aid kit. "How did this happen?" Mary would ask as she was attending the wound.

"That dumb-shit Johnny hit the back-end of my quad and it flipped and landed on me." Don replied.

"You may need to go to the hospital. You may need stitches. I don't think you hit anything major, but by the way it was bleeding, we need to go, just to be sure."

"Fuck that. I ain't going to no fucking hospital. If I am gonna die, it won't be there. It will be right here in my home. Just sew it closed if you gotta, but I ain't going there." Don said. He was always kind of a stubborn s.o.b.

"Dam it, Don. You are NOT going to die on my couch either." Mary said as she got the needle and thread ready. She took out her lighter and heated the needle with the flame.

"I am gonna go outside for a bit" I said as I realized why she was heating the needle. "I need a drink, you probably do to, Don."

"Get the vodka for me." Mary said.

"Do you really think that's a good idea, right now, Mary? Shouldn't you be sober before you sew me up?" Don said.

"While *your* stupid ass is half drunk? No. It isn't for me, genius. It's for your wound. Wait, I think there may be some rubbing alcohol under the sink"

I checked under the sink and there was a half empty bottle of isopropyl alcohol. I then grabbed the bottle of vodka from the pantry and brought both to Mary. She took the cap off the vodka, handed it to Don and said, "Take a big drink."

Don took two huge gulps directly from the bottle and handed the bottle back to her. She set the vodka down and opened the isopropyl. She looked him in the eye and said, "Ready?"

"Do it." Don replied as his hands gripped the couch.

"On three," Mary said as Don took a deep breath, "One."

Mary poured isopropyl directly onto the wound as she said one. "AWWW!" screamed Don and then took a deep breath through his teeth. I went around Mary to get the bottle of vodka. I am not ashamed to say that I wasn't too proud to not take a few big drinks myself. I went to the front door and went outside, then I fired up a cigarette and thought about how lucky Don was to be alive.

Don's wound eventually healed and he was able to fully recover. The next day Mary took him to the hospital, despite much resistance from Don, just to get him checked out. No major damage, but I imagine he has a gnarly cool scar.

Chapter 30:

Colorado

In early April 2008, Don (from the Quads story) calls me and says he is working in Colorado and needs help. He offers me a job as an iron worker. I thought about it for like five seconds and I said yes.

Iron work is no joke. It rates as the third most dangerous job in the world. On average, two workers are killed per year. The missed workdays caused by major and minor injuries caused by this work are staggering. However, when you are taking dangerous work you are compensated through an equally staggering pay scale. I decided that this would be a great way to get caught up on my bills and the financial jump would be worth the risk.

It was May 1st, 2008 when I moved to Colorado. This was going to be a fresh start for me. Getting out of Phoenix, at the time, seemed just like what the doctor ordered. To add to that prescription, I was going to be making $26 an hour, plus $30 a day per diem. While I made good money before, I felt live this new career was going to be the key to reaching my first million.

Colorado was a major change for me in that when I got to Denver, it was really cold. Let me put this into perspective for you. Phoenix was in the mid 90 degrees Fahrenheit range in May, whereas Denver was mid 50s during the day, and it snowed once during the first month I was there.

The work I was doing in Colorado was tough. We would basically get to work just as the sun was rising and would not be done for the day until sunset, sometimes well after. I went from working in office buildings and hospitals to working in what was basically farms. The project was to build huge windmills. My crew was responsible for unloading the blades and rotors from the trucks that would deliver them to the site and place them on the ground. There were six of us plus a mobile crane operator and the crane spotter. There was another crew that would off load the cylinders. Then, yet another crew would build the windmills. This is extremely dangerous work. On average, three people are killed each year doing this and injuries on the job are numerous.

Another issue we faced daily was the wind. When we would off load the materials for the windmills, occasionally we would have a slight breeze. Remember, these materials are made for catching the wind. If the wind picked up over 8 m.p.h. we had to stop work to hope that it would die back down. This area was chosen for the windmills because of the wind, so this happened so often that somedays we would only be able to off load one or two blades, others we would be able to off load every truck that came to the site.

During the weekends or when weather was not idea for offloading, I had the chance to have some fun in Colorado. One thing I noticed almost immediately is that beer in this state is very week. Most beer is 5% alcohol, but in Colorado beer is 3.2%. This makes you want to drink more beer to achieve the same effect that you would have achieved anywhere else. My suspicion is this is to make citizens spend more money in order to increase sales and, by proxy, increase sales tax revenue for the site. I have no doubt that this was achieve under the guise of preventing people from becoming too drunk. The adverse happened with me as I switched from drinking beer to drinking mixed whiskey drinks.

The fourth weekend I was in Colorado I decided I wanted My Angel to come and spend a weekend with me.

She agreed, so I bought her a round trip plane ticket and drove to Denver to pick her up. Here is where I started to have a problem with Don. I was paying him $400 a week to rent a room from him in the house that he and his wife was renting in Loveland. Yes, you read that right, $400 a week! At that rate, I shouldn't have to ask permission to bring my girlfriend in, but he and his wife had a problem with it because they had their 15-year-old daughter there as well. In hindsight, and with me having raised girls of my own now, I get it, but still, $400 a week and I have to get a hotel room for two days? I was pissed, but that is life I guess.

I also had the opportunity to explore parts of Colorado. We drove into the Rockies one weekend to Blackhawk. Blackhawk had many casinos at that time, including what was called Fitzgerald's at that time. Naturally, we were drinking and gambling the entire time. Whenever it was that I went to my hotel room I remember looking out the window and seeing a large amount of snow.

I thought to myself, "That's not good." How are we going to get back to Loveland in the morning so we can get to the job site the next day. Well, to my complete surprise, the next morning the snow had completely melted and all that was left was water flowing away. It was one of the craziest things I have ever witnessed.

By mid-June that year the windmill job was winding down and there was some discussion as to where the next job would be. Don mentioned New York more than once and I would get excited at the prospect of seeing a state that I had never been to. To top it off, I've always been a history buff and New York is filled with American history. Unfortunately, this was not to be.

At the end of June, I decided I wanted to come back to Arizona for a few days and visit my family, and I called My Angel to say I was coming back for a few days. She was excited. The only person I told I was coming in my family was my little brother. I booked my flight for July 3rd and return on July 7th. The morning I was supposed to fly out to Phoenix I got called in to the construction office. Don was sitting in the boss's office with Jim, who was the main boss for the jobsite. Jim said, "Come on in and have a seat please. We want to talk to you."

I found this kind of scene unsettling and reminded me of movies where someone is giving someone else some bad news. "What's going on guys?" I inquired with a fear in my voice as to what the answer is going to be.

Don said, "Can we get you a cup of coffee or anything?"

"I'm good, thanks."

"You know we think you have been doing just a fantastic job here." Jim said.

I interrupted saying, "Glad to hear it."

Jim continued, "Yeah, but this job is starting to wind down and, well we have to let some people go."

I said, "Are you firing me? I thought you guys were happy with my work?"

At this, Don looks like he wants to cry. He looks at his feet, folds his hands and I can see he has become quite uncomfortable. I thought 'Don, what the fuck? Didn't you say you were going to take care of me? Didn't you swear to my Dad that you had my back? Don, you piece of shit'.

Jim goes on, "Oh my God, no, we are not firing you, but we can't keep you on the payroll any longer, so we are laying you off."

Layoffs were something I had only read about. Wasn't that what happened during the Depression? "What does *that* mean?" I asked.

"It means that you can collect unemployment benefits and we are going to pay you out for your vacation time accrued. I would like it very much if we could re-hire you once the next job starts, but that could be four to six months."

"Oh. I thought I did something wrong." I started chuckling just a bit. "Don, you ok man?"

Don finally looked up from his feet at me. "Yea, I'm alright. I just feel bad right now because I brought you here and thought we would have more jobs lined up for you. Guess its ok, huh?"

I thought about what he just said for a moment before I answered. "Yea, its ok. I'm actually flying back to Phoenix later today. I guess I better pack all my stuff, not just enough for a few days."

"Let's step outside and have a smoke." Don said, "That way Jim can have his office back. Thanks Jim."

"Yes, thanks Jim" I said. Don and I stepped outside and lit a cigarette each. As we stood there I took in the beauty of this Colorado countryside for the last time. As I took it in, Don still looked a bit sad.

"So, you are leaving and going back to Phoenix? When were you going to tell me?" Don asked.

"I was going to tell you after work today, my flight is at 7 tonight so there would have been plenty of time. When did you know I was getting laid off?"

"Yesterday. They told me not to say anything until Jim could talk to you."

"Wow. That's a heavy secret to keep. And, when I booked my flight it was only for four days. Now, am I coming back?"

"I'll see what I can find out. In the meantime, enjoy the down time." Don said.

"Ok, but for how long. I can't just sit around my Dad's house indefinitely."

"Give me a couple of days, I'll let you know if you should come back to Colorado or if you should stay in Phoenix."

I said, "Sounds good." We shook hands and I got in the car and drove the 60-minute drive back to Loveland. I went into the house and started packing all my things, which conveniently fit into two suitcases. I asked Don's wife if she could drive me to Denver, since I was flying out and probably not going to be back anytime soon. She agreed, so I poured myself a drink.

I got to the Denver airport around 3:00 pm, checked in with the airline and found my way to the lounge in the terminal. I had just enough time before boarding my flight to get good and drunk, the only way to fly! When I got on the plane I quickly passed out. Apparently, I snore a good bit as the flight attendant woke me up a few times to make sure I was breathing. When I landed in Phoenix my brother was there waiting. I got my bags from the baggage claim and he drive me to my Dad's house, where I found my Dad passed out in his recliner. I woke him up to say I was back, he smiled and asked me why. I explained what happened and he said something like "good."

After this, I asked my brother if he wanted to go to the casino with me, to which he said no. I borrowed his car and drove myself where I would lose about $200 and drink until well after the sun came up. I somehow found my way home and passed out. Most of the time after the flight home was hazy. The day was the Fourth of July, so that meant plenty more drinking coming up.

My Angel called me several times on the Fourth of July, but I was in no shape to be a boyfriend at that point, so I called her back on the Fifth. Obviously, I had some explaining to do. After many apologies and a crab leg dinner at Red Lobster (which was our first date spot year's previous), she forgave me and we made up. Don called me on the Sixth and told me that the other jobs are delayed so I probably should just stay in Phoenix for the time being. To which I agreed.

Being a low-voltage technician (or any tradesman, for that matter) has a few benefits. While I am no longer active as a technician, should I need to I could find a job as a technician in that trade, even today. However, at this point in my life (2007) I was in no hurry to re-enter that trade, so I decided I would stay on unemployment for the time being. Another benefit of having a trade is that every once in a while someone may ask you to help on their job and pay you cash.

Chapter 31:

Unemployment

Being on government assistance can be depressing. I grew up with the "have something to do to give life meaning" mentality. I was always one of the first students to arrive at school all through elementary and high schools.

When I started working, I had the 15-minute rule of thumb: If I am there 15 minutes early, I am on time. I really love having something to do to give my life meaning.

While I was unemployed, you really start to go into a depression the longer you cannot find a job and look to fill the void with anything. I have a sympathy for those who become addicted to drugs because that could have very easily become me at this point. Then, in the middle of August this year, Don would call me again and briefly raise my hopes.

"Hey, how are you doing?" Don asked.

"Just trying to keep myself busy, you know. Trying to enjoy this downtime, but I'm ready to get back to work. Anything good happening?"

Don was silent for a brief moment. "Well, it sucks, but unfortunately the jobs are still delayed."

I asked, "For how much longer?"

"Not too sure" Don replied, "but I'll keep you posted and keep mentioning your mane every chance I get."

"What about you? Are you working? Did they lay you off too?"

Again, silence. "Ah, well no. I am still working here in Colorado as the job winds down."

I said, "Don, the job was winding down at the beginning of July, now we are in mid-August, so what the hell's going on?"

"Yea, well there are just some technical loose ends here for management. There isn't any more off loads to building going on. Nothing really for you to do." Don said.

"Ok, I tell you what. If I do not hear from you by the first of September, I am going to have to start looking for another job." I said, rather calmly for the situation.

"That's probably not a bad idea. Not that we don't want you back, but I don't know if these other locations are going to be ready before the first of the new year. Sorry about that." Don said.

I replied, "Well, thanks for the actual head's up. I gotta go." And I hung up the phone as quickly as I could.

Here is where my friend Don exits my story. After this phone call I have never spoken to him again.

Unemployment continued for me until late October 2007, when I spoke with my uncle, who had no idea I was back in Phoenix. He later spoke with his boss and they soon offered me my old job back at the company that I had left in May. Perhaps here would have been a great time to thank God for all the blessings I have received up to this point in my life. Nope, it was not yet meant to be as I was so far lost from God that I had not even the slightest regard to God.

After a few paychecks from my new company I had a few options. My Angel wanted me to get a house with her and for us to make things super serious, but I did not want that domesticated life just yet, so instead I moved out of my Dad's place and found a 2-bedroom apartment. Why did I get 2 bedrooms? Because this was the only apartment at the complex I wanted that was on the ground floor. I paid an extra $50 a month for it, too. I gotta say, there is something to be said for living on the ground floor of an apartment complex. I do not like climbing stairs after a hard day's work, just to get into my home. I do not like carrying heavy furniture upstairs only to move out at some point and have to carry it back down.

One small note here, because of my decision to move into an apartment and not get serious with My Angel I almost lost her forever. She ended up buying a house and started getting serious with someone else. In hindsight, this was a real turning point for me, almost losing someone that had really been there for me through some of my darkest days.

The apartment and single life were dismal. I thought I would enjoy my time being alone and on my own again, but ultimately, I was lonely. Did I rekindle my relationship with God? No, it was not yet in the cards for me to get back with the Lord. In this apartment I would spend almost every moment I wasn't working with a beer in my hand and playing online poker. I discovered that I have a talent for poker, as long as I am not too drunk. When I reached a certain point (probably near alcohol poisoning), I would start to lose. When you are highly intoxicated and you lose, you think, "Well if I play just *one* more game I could start a comeback". Unfortunately, that one more would turn into ten or twenty and that comeback would end up being hundreds of dollars lost.

This scenario would almost be daily: I wake up, get showered and dressed, go to work, get off work, stop and get a case of beer, back to the apartment and drink case of beer, pass out, repeat. This would go on for almost ten months. Kind of reminds me of my childhood routine, except for the beers.

Chapter 32:

October of 2008

My Angel and I would speak again. First, the usual 'how have you been?' 'What's been going on with you?' 'Miss me?' These sorts of questions we would discuss at first, but then I took a radical, yet logical step:

"You know, we have been going back and forth for nearly seven years now. I am getting tired of all these ups and downs, aren't you?" I asked.

"Well of course I am. But every time I think we are going to get serious you go and do something stupid." My Angel told me.

"I know. I just think you and I are going to have to go all the way or just end it and go no way further. This back and forth is just too much. I think we either need to move in together or we will never have a chance."

There was a long silence on her end. "What about my children?"

I said, "What about them? I've always had a place in my heart for them."

"That's not how you seemed when you would go out drinking." She was right, I never had made time to spend with her kids, but I never had kids before and didn't know what it was all about.

"All I can say is I think I can do better."

"Well, you are going to have to if you have this to happen. Let me sleep on it and I will call you tomorrow." My Angel said.

"Alright, till then." I replied.

"If this is going to go forward, you better figure out the plan."

I asked, "What does that mean?"

Again, silence. Then, "Well, if we are going to live together, you better figure a way. What happens with you lease? How do we move you in and are you prepared to act like a father?" My Angel had two girls before she met me.

"I will do whatever it takes at this point. I love you and the girls. If I have to break my lease and bite that bullet, then that's what I have to do." I responded.

My Angel said, "Well, think it through, though. Wouldn't your lease be up in two months anyway? What if it costs less to stay those two months than to break your lease? Find out."

She always has a way of speaking that makes some sense to me. Later that day, I would get back to the apartment complex and head to the management's office. I explained to the lady at the front desk what I am trying to do and what is the best way to proceed. Of course, I'm told to have a seat and wait for her boss. Why are the simplest questions always the most difficult to get answers to?

What I could only describe as a burly man would come out from the back office. "I understand you want to break your lease, young man?"

Why do people insist on speaking condescending to people younger than themselves? I replied, "Not necessarily, I am just trying to examine my options and make the best decision based on what those options are."

"Well let's see what we can do. Please step into my office." he said.

My thought was 'about time, conversation should have happened in private anyway'. I rose from the chair and followed this man into his office. He was wearing a dingy yellow shirt with a black tie with blue stripes, brown khakis and well-polished shoes. He was slightly balding and I think he would have looked better in the squad room of a police station rather than managing an apartment complex. He sat in a black cushioned chair and motioned me to sit in the stationary, rather uncomfortable looking chair on the opposite side of the desk. I sat down and waited for him to begin.

"So, why don't you tell me what's going on and why you want to break your lease." He said.

I started, "Well my girlfriend and I are trying to move in with each other and me living here is detrimental to that goal. I just need to know if it's going to cost more if I break my lease or may the remaining months on it."

The burly man replies, "I see. Well, why don't you have her move in with you here, we'd love to have her here too."

My nice demeanor suddenly changed for the briefest of moments and I almost said 'I don't see how that is any of your business.' However, what I actually said was "Oh, that would be great, I've had a good experience here, but we are buying a house."

"Ah. Congratulations."

"Thanks, we are super excited." I'm so full of shit in this conversation.

"Well, give me a moment. I see your rent in $850 a month and you have two months left on your lease, so $1,700 for two months." The burly man said.

I said, "Ok."

The burly man reaches to his left and starts typing numbers into a large calculator with a receipt tape. A minute or two later "To break your lease comes to about $1,690. Plus, whatever cleaning we have to do to rent it again, which I can't calculate until we inspect. So, and this is just my opinion here, but if it was me, I would stay and finish out your lease. You are young and don't need that black mark on your history."

That is the second time this mother fucker stuck his nose in my business and it is starting to piss me off. "So, what you are saying is it will cost me a little less money to break the lease as it will to stay. Alright, thanks." I start to stand up.

The burly man says, "Hold on there, son. There's more to this than just money. It will also go on your credit report."

Now this asshole has seriously pissed me off with his looking down at me by calling me 'son'. I got up and moved toward his office door, stopped at the doorway and said, "Alright man, listen. I am not your son and its really none of your fucking business whether or not we move in here or not. I don't give a damn about my credit report and

I just came here to get my options and you have been extremely rude and condescending to me."

"I didn't mean to come off as rude and I apologize if you are offended." The burly man replied. "I am just trying to help you out here. You do not have to get so angry when someone is helping.

I said, "Fuck you." And gave him the middle finger. "You can keep your kind of fucking help and shove it right up your ass."

I went out the door and left the apartment complex office to return to my apartment. I called My Angel. No answer, so I grabbed a beer from the fridge. Ten minutes or so pass and my phone rings. It's My Angel. "Hello" I said.

"So, what happened with the lease?" she asked.

"I think I'm gonna have to move out anyway. The manager here is an asshole and he really pissed me off so I told him 'Fuck you'." I explained.

Silence for a moment. "Why did you do that?"

"He was treating me like a child. He talking about moving you here and credit reports and shit. Fuck all that."

My Angel said, "I need you to calm down, please. Grab a beer if you need to. Do not allow stupid people and their stupid opinions to affect you like that."

"I already have one and I'm trying to calm down."

"Good, can you just tell me the options?"

"I'm sorry, I know. Yea, so the options are the same, they charge about two months' rent to break the lease and I owe two months on my lease. So, if we want, the best course is to break my lease." I said. "If that I what you still want."

My Angel said, "I am going to have to call you back later tonight. Please do not drink too much tonight."

"Alright." I said. We hung up and I finished my beer. I though I should start packing, but having another beer and then another while playing online poker seemed more important. I am going to tell you straight, I hate moving. There is nothing fun about it and, in my experience, people say they will help are no where to be found on moving day. For example, growing up my Dad would force me and my brother to assist my Aunt Michelle and Uncle Dan in moving them in and out of at least three places. My Dad would always say that they will owe you when you have to move and you will be happy to have helped them at that point. He was wrong. When I moved into my first apartment or second or this one, they never helped. I had no reason to expect anyone to lift a finger with this move either.

After my third beer I received a text message from My Angel that read:

Go ahead and start packing. I will call U-Haul in the morning and see how much to rent a truck. So EXCITING!

I replied: Sounds Good!

I spent the rest of the evening packing my stuff. Despite living in this apartment for ten months most of my stuff was still in Tupperware boxes in the spare room, so I only had to pack my clothes, take apart my bed and box up dishes and stuff of a household nature. I went to sleep on my couch that night, largely ready for the move. I got a phone call around 8:00 a.m. from My Angel. "Hello, beautiful." I answered.

"Good morning. Did you pack last night?"

"Yes. I think I am pretty much all set here. Did you call U-Haul?" I asked.

"I just got off the phone. It's gonna be about $100 for the day, can you get out of there today?" she asked.

I replied, "I think so, its gonna be tight because I have no help loading my stuff."

"What all do you have?"

"Well, the biggest thing is probably my couch. I took my bed apart last night, so that is piece mail to load and my entertainment center is light without the T.V. in it." I said. T.V.s were still pretty heavy and bulky in 2008 and mine was almost ten years old. "Everything else is boxed up, like dishes and other stuff."

"What about your *other* stuff?" She asked. I'll be honest with you, I had a pretty amazing collection of adult magazines and movies that had grown to incredible proportions. I had Playboys, Penthouse, Hustlers, VHS tapes, and DVDs (full movie and interactive which were new at the time). There was easily a thousand dollars' worth, but when we first started discussing moving in together she had made it VERY clear that she did not want that in her house. Which I understood that having young children 'accidentally' find them could devastate the child in many ways, not the least of which was their lost innocence. I told her that it wasn't a problem to get rid of.

"That stuff is gone. I gave it to (a co-worker whose name is not important). He was happy to get that big box of smut." I said.

"Good, I really wouldn't mind you keeping it, but if the girls ever came across it, even by accident, they would never look at you the same again." She told me.

I said, "Its all good. Better off without it. What time do I get the U-Haul?"

"9:00 a.m. is when they said you could pick it up. Its right over by Metro Center Mall."

"Oh, Ok. I know where that U-Haul is, right on the corner of the freeway. I'll take a shower and head that way now."

"I'm sorry I can't help you load up. It just I have somethings to do today that can't wait." She said.

"Yea, yea. Whatever, lazy ass." I joked with her. "See you later."

From here I showered, dressed, got a quick bite to eat at Sonic and went to U-Haul. The man there was very polite and I got the truck. I drove back to my apartment and began loading. I spent the next eight hours loading what I could by myself. The last thing to load was the couch. I struggled to get it out the door, but somehow, I got it through, alone. When I got it to the truck ramp I started to think about how to get it up and in. As I was about to attempt it I hear a voice, "Do you need a hand?"

I turned to see a thirty something, skinny and bald-headed Hispanic man. "Wow, you have great timing. I was just about to try to muscle this up myself. Yes, I would appreciate it."

"No problem." He says and then he helps me load the couch. "Moving out, huh?"

"Yes. I am moving in with my girlfriend. You live in one of these apartments?" I asked.

"Yea. I live on the second floor right above you, I think." He says.

"Oh wow. Do you have a big dog or something?"

He looks at me for a second and says, "Yes I do, a Great Dane. How did you know?"

I replied, "Well, at least once a day I would hear a loud bang on the ceiling which I assume is a dog or someone jumping off the couch."

He laughs and says, "I'm sorry about that. Guess I never realized that these floors were so thin."

"Oh, no problem. Since I've lived here I've always wondered what the hell was making that noise." I told the man. "Well, thanks for the help. Too bad we didn't get a chance to know each other while I lived here."

He replied, "Yea, man. Wish we could have hung out. Oh well, good luck."

With that, I was packed. I walked back in the apartment to double check that I had gotten everything. I took a brief moment to look around and thought about how my single life days had now come to an end. I really took it in that this was genuinely an adult move and felt a sense of pride.

I closed the door and took a moment to take in what exactly was happening. As I closed the door it was a metaphor on closing this portion of my odyssey. The part of my life involving partying and the single life was now at an end. In a way, when I closed that door for the last time I had closed the life of a young man and was stepping into adulthood. When I got to the U-Haul truck, I thought for a moment about throwing the apartment keys in a dumpster, but I chose to do the right thing and I took them to the office.

When I got to the office and told the lady at the desk that I was giving her my keys because I was breaking my lease. She had the oddest look on her face as I did. As if, when people break their lease they never bring their keys, let alone be polite. I had a huge sense of pride in that I did the right thing for this complex. After that, I was on my way to my new life with My Angel and her girls. You would think that now would have been a good time to thank God for the new change in my life, but that was not yet to come.